# HEXES AND THE HAUNTED HOUSE

### A WILLIAMS WITCH MYSTERY
### BOOK FOUR

## ELOISE EVERHART

ALORIUM PUBLISHING

PB ISBN: 978-1-962759-03-8

Author: Eloise Everhart

Editors: Rashida Breen and Angela McRae

Cover design by GetCovers

# CHAPTER 1

I stared up at Meredith Walker's house. Grace and the Retirees crowded around me. Sarah, Betty, and Agnes were silent, their necks craned as they studied the home. We had stopped by the night before. There was something sinister about the boards haphazardly covering the windows and the way the house seemed to lean over the street. In the dark, none of us could muster the courage to take the first step inside. We had stood frozen on the front steps until Agnes suggested we come back when it was light out. We hoped it would be less intimidating in the day. Somehow, it had gotten worse.

The plan made me uneasy. After Grace had found the key to the house in a box of mementos that had belonged to Sarah's mother, she was laser focused on getting inside. All her dreams, and the stories the Retirees remembered about the origins of the curse that plagued all our families, hinted that it started there. The place felt cursed. Everything around it was bright and cheery, but the house seemed to suck in light. It was as if it had a permanent gloom hanging over it.

I tried to visualize the house as it was in the picture Grace had found. It was a black-and-white shot, but I liked to imagine the home was painted a nice beige. It was a two-story craftsman sitting at the top of a hill in the heart of Point Pleasant on Whidbey Island. Broken windows along the ground indicated it had a basement, which was uncommon on that side of the Cascades. I held onto the image of a tan house with a picket fence and tried to force a smile onto my face.

"All right, ladies. Are you ready to see if the key works?" I asked.

"No." Agnes wrapped her arms around her. "I know it's the middle of winter, but I swear when I take a step closer, it gets noticeably colder. It's frigid enough already."

"That's called the shade," Betty quipped, although she didn't move any nearer herself.

"I know the difference between shade and this feeling," Agnes shot back. "And this is different. It feels wrong here."

"This is the best lead we've got. Meredith was a member of your mother's coven. She disappeared the same year the curse started, and her house has been vacant ever since. It can't be a coincidence. Answers are inside. Do you honestly think we'll be able to figure out what happened if we don't go in?" Grace asked.

"I've lived long enough not knowing." Sarah draped her arm around Agnes's shoulder. "Is this really necessary?"

"Well, if you won't go in, then I guess I'll do it on my own." Grace straightened her shoulders and took a few steps forward. After the third step, she faltered and scampered back. "Just as soon as the sun comes all the way up."

I tried not to laugh. The house had a presence, and all of us could feel it. I couldn't blame Grace for not having the nerve to go in alone. None of us had the night before. I wasn't sure I had the confidence to go in with a group.

"It *is* all the way up," Sarah whispered.

We stood in silence, staring at the house. We knew almost nothing about Meredith Walker. There were a lot of photos of her with my great-grandmother's coven, so we assumed she was a member. But we didn't know what happened to her. The Retirees' mothers had never brought her up in conversation. She was in photo after photo until she wasn't. She vanished around the time the rest of the coven was cursed; a curse that had gone down the familial lines ever since. Without going into the house, it was impossible for us to know whether she'd started the curse or if she was its first victim. Like Grace said, we couldn't ignore the timeline. It really was our best shot at finding answers to the all-important questions: Who cursed us? Why did they curse us? And how could we break it?

My family's curse hit my daughter Grace especially hard. We both had the Sight, but hers made life almost unbearable. Her nightmares kept her awake most nights. She couldn't touch anything without feeling the emotions of whoever had touched an object last. And that frequently became a vicious feedback loop as her emotions fed into what she was feeling until she was shaking and crying on the floor. It had forced her to drop out of college and move in with me. My ex-husband was not pleased, especially since she couldn't explain what was wrong. He wouldn't understand her being a witch. So instead, he blamed me, since what he labeled as her emotional breakdown had happened soon after I filed for divorce. He was too much of a narcissist to realize I left him because I finally realized I wasn't happy and couldn't be happy with someone who didn't really care about me.

I gritted my teeth. The Retirees might be okay with not knowing, but I had to. For my daughter. I squared my shoulders and held my hand out.

"The key," I said.

Grace dropped it into my hand.

I strode across the street. Grace and the Retirees scampered after me. They huddled together a few feet behind me and shuffled forward as a group. *For Grace. I have to know for*

*Grace. Stop being a coward. It's only a house.* I peered up at the craftsman home as I ascended the broken concrete stairs. *A creepy, possibly haunted house.*

My hands shook as I pushed the key into the lock on the front door. Despite the layers of rust on the lock, the key slid into place easily. I swallowed and looked back at my daughter. The Retirees clustered around her, all having donned matching puffy jackets. Somehow, in the house's shadow, they seemed fragile. They had never looked weak to me before. Even with their graying hair and deep-set laugh lines, they exuded energy. But right then, they huddled around Grace, giving support and receiving it in return. They clutched each other as I turned to the door and twisted the key in the lock.

It clicked. My heart skipped a beat, and I held my breath as I pushed the door inward.

The inside was trashed. Beer bottles littered the floor, and graffiti covered the walls. I let out the breath I had been holding. With the door open, the knot of fear inside me unwound. Over the years, I had inspected a lot of abandoned properties owned by banks. The house reminded me of so many of them. Empty houses became magnets for kids looking for a place to party or for the homeless in search of a place to crash for the night, protected from the elements. That space was no different.

I hovered in the doorway. *If it's no different, then why don't I want to go inside?* The hairs on the back of my neck hadn't gone down. I counted backward from ten and stepped through the door when I hit number one. A shiver went through me, and the knot of fear in my stomach tightened again.

Whispers filled the air. I couldn't make out any words. It was like a whispered conversation in another room, no one word distinct. I steadied myself and took another step inside.

"What do you see?" Betty asked.

The group hadn't moved. They still clung to each other a few feet from the porch.

"Graffiti."

"So somebody's been inside?" Grace pulled away from the Retirees and inched her way up the steps.

"Several somebodies, by the look of it." I nudged the edge of an abandoned blanket.

I waited in the middle of the living room. The unnerving feeling that had settled over me when I stepped inside hadn't gone away. My skin crawled. A voice in the back of my head screamed for me to get out, to run away and never come back. My hands clenched involuntarily at my sides. The pressure of my nails digging into my palms grounded me. I focused on that sensation while I waited.

Grace stepped through the front door and gasped as she crossed the threshold.

"Do you feel that?" she asked.

I nodded.

She darted toward me and grabbed my arm. Her gloved fingers dug into my skin as she wrapped herself around my shoulder, burying her face in my hair.

A few seconds later, the Retirees followed her inside and closed the door behind them, probably to keep any passersby from accidentally coming in after us. They stood as a group in the dim light.

"This definitely feels like a place where a curse could have happened," Agnes said.

Sarah and Betty spoke over each other as they described what they were feeling. A tightening of the chest. Insects crawling across their skin. A faint whisper in the air.

"Do you know what they're saying?" I asked.

The Retirees shook their heads in unison.

"We wouldn't be here if you hadn't..." Grace pulled away from me and stood in the middle of the room, swaying with her eyes closed. "You did this."

"Hadn't what?" I asked.

Grace shook her head. "I can't make it out. Just the occasional word here or there. It's all blurring together."

"All right. We're here. We made it inside. Let's be quick about this. Look for clues about what caused the curse, and then get out," Betty said, stepping away from the group. "Keep each other in sight. I'll go left with Agnes. Sarah, you and Grace go right. Dani, pick a direction, but don't go too far. We don't know what could be in a place like this."

The tension in my shoulders eased a fraction. I was used to Betty acting with confidence. Seeing her step back into a leadership role reassured me. It couldn't be that bad if Betty was confident.

The groups dispersed. Grace took her gloves off and hesitantly touched the wall. I followed suit. One of our most useful gifts was psychometry. It was our ability to read the emotional residue left behind by whoever had touched something last or, if the object was involved in something impactful, the most important emotions connected to the object. Grace was better at it than I was. She picked up more than just the emotions. Sometimes, she saw stuff as well. I had to cast spells to see anything. My latent ability to read an object began and ended with emotion. But then again, her visions were always of the past while mine were of the future. The future couldn't leave an emotional residue. It hadn't happened yet. While it was only a small silver lining, she never had to deal with visions of impending doom, only doom that had long passed.

I kept the group in my peripheral vision as I stepped farther into the house. It was an older home, so it had more walls than a recent construction. The kitchen and dining room had a wall separating them. Doors led from room to room, with a long hallway running down the center of the house, with a flight of stairs at the end.

Touching the walls left an oily sensation on my skin. It

was like nothing I had ever experienced. The wrongness of the place made my teeth ache. *For Grace. I have to know what happened, for Grace. Her nightmares won't end until we know.* I forced myself to keep my finger on the wall as I continued down the hallway toward the stairs.

Each inch of curling wallpaper was filled with a mixture of rage and fear. *How could anyone hang out here?* In the doorway to my left, Betty peered around the kitchen. Agnes stood next to her with her arms wrapped around her body.

I forced myself forward. I stopped at the foot of the stairs and craned my head. There were no lights at the top of the stairs. All the windows had been boarded up. The weak sunlight filtering in through the cracks between the boards didn't reach that far. I fumbled in my pocket and pulled out my cell phone for a light. My hands shook as I turned it on and took my first step onto the stairs.

"Ouch," Grace hissed behind me.

I turned toward her and froze midmovement.

A woman had appeared at the top of the stairs.

I swallowed and shifted my gaze to her. She floated an inch above the top step. Her hair swirled behind her. She gave off an eerie green light, which allowed me to see the space around her. It was a standard landing. A table stood behind her, and I could see it only because she was completely translucent.

The woman let out a wordless wail.

I stumbled back and tried to cover my ears. It didn't help. The sound wasn't coming from her. It was coming from inside my head.

The Retirees ran into the living room behind me, their hands over their ears. We all stood there, staring up at the woman as her expressions shifted. She settled on rage.

The woman flew down the stairs toward me. I took a step back. My foot came down on a bottle, and I fell backward. Pain shot through my body as I landed hard on my tailbone.

Betty grabbed me by my shoulders and yanked me toward the front door as the woman floated closer. I scrambled backward across the room as Betty pulled me along. Agnes darted ahead and opened the front door.

The wailing grew louder the closer the woman came. I couldn't look away from her. Even when I had been staring down Tina's killer, I had never seen someone so filled with rage. It was in every inch of her body. It consumed her. The emotions of the house shifted with her. With every touch of my hand, the rage grew.

My hand found the lip of the front door, and I scooted outside as Betty and Agnes scrambled out of the way of the group. Sarah and Grace stumbled out after me. Agnes lunged and closed the door and locked it.

"What was that?" I whispered.

I didn't wait for anyone to answer. We scrambled down the stairs and fled to my car. The Retirees piled into the back seat. Grace threw herself into the passenger seat and hugged her hand to her body.

"I don't feel good." Grace wavered in her seat and slumped against the dash.

"What happened?" I pulled her up to look at her. Grace's skin was clammy. Her eyes moved rapidly under the closed lids.

"She got a splinter," Sarah said. "Do you have tweezers?"

"At my office." *A splinter.* I blinked. A piece of that house was under her skin. She wouldn't be able to get away from the emotional feedback loop. It would just continue building. *What happens if it's in there too long?* My gran told me that when I was a kid, I was comatose for a week when the Sight overwhelmed me. I wouldn't let that happen to Grace.

# CHAPTER 2

I white-knuckled it the entire drive to my office. Grace sat slumped against the passenger window, mumbling incoherently. A five-minute drive had never felt so long.

I screeched to a stop right outside the front door and jumped out of the car. The Retirees piled out after me and grabbed Grace. She was half awake. I dashed ahead to unlock the doors. She toddled groggily between Agnes and Betty as they guided her through the front door. They trailed me through the lobby and into my office. The Retirees helped Grace to a chair and lingered around her as I grabbed the first aid kit from the back wall.

Our sudden entrance woke up my cat, Charlie, who had been dozing on the front windowsill. He yawned and stretched as I fumbled with the kit. His pupils narrowed to slits, and he leaped from his perch and vaulted across the room and onto Grace's chest. He rammed his fluffy head against her cheek and wrapped his paws around her neck as I darted to her.

I handed my cell phone to Sarah. "Hold the light steady."

Sarah hovered over Grace's shoulder, holding the light.

I pushed my glasses up and leaned over Grace's hand. She

whimpered as I touched her skin. Not only was Grace dealing with the feedback from the splinter, but she also had to feel my worry. *It's going to be okay.* I blinked back a tear. *She's going to be okay. She won't end up like I did. Grace is strong.* Charlie shoved his head against her, purring into her ear.

"Good boy," I whispered.

I grabbed the tweezer from the first aid box and turned her hand over in mine until I found the splinter. It was slender, about a quarter of an inch long, and wedged under the skin on her index finger. I grabbed the end of the piece of wood and pulled. It came loose on the second tug. I released her hand and threw the splinter into the trash.

The second it was out, Grace's breathing evened. She shuddered and wrapped her arms around Charlie. The Retirees let out their breaths and slumped into the other chairs in the room. I stood, shakily, and sagged into my seat behind my desk.

"Are you okay?" I asked.

Grace buried her head in Charlie's fur. "I will be."

"That was… intense." I wrapped my arms around myself. The adrenaline was wearing off. I desperately wanted to hug my daughter, but right then, she needed as few things as possible touching her. *If only Chris were here. If only Chris knew.* I let the thought trail off before my mind went down another rabbit hole. I would have to tell Chris before things got serious between us, but I wasn't ready. Not yet. *What if he can't handle it?* I shook my head, chasing away the fear of another failed relationship.

"I'm getting used to it." Grace straightened in her chair and pulled out her gloves. She slipped them onto her hands and resumed petting Charlie. "So, when are we going back?"

"Back?" I bolted to my feet. "How can you be talking about going back? After what that place did to you? What even was that?"

"You know what that was. A feedback loop." Grace glowered. "Caused by the curse. Yes, this time, it was caused by the house. But it wasn't the first time. And it sure won't be the last, unless we do something about it."

I swayed in place. Grace was right. *We have to go back. She can't live a normal life if she can't touch anything, or anyone, without risking her sanity.* The only way for her to get a handle on her powers for good was to end the curse that was making them go haywire.

"All right. So we go back. What do we do about that woman?" I asked.

"If it even was a woman," Agnes said.

My head swiveled to her, my eyes wide. It hadn't occurred to me that it could have been anything but a person. It looked like one. An eerie, green, glowing, translucent one but still a woman.

"It could be any number of things, really," Sarah agreed.

"A ghost." Betty ticked the possibilities off on her fingers. "Part of the house's security."

"A spell echo," Agnes added.

"A cruel practical joke," Sarah said.

"Ghosts are real?" My knees shook. It was one thing to know that witches were real, but adding ghosts to the list made my world feel so much bigger and scarier than before. I flopped into my chair.

"Oh yes," Betty said.

Agnes picked up where she'd left off. "Usually not visible, though."

"You have to know what to look for," Sarah concluded.

"Okay. So how do we figure it out?" I asked as I fidgeted in my chair. I had too much nervous energy. Even though my legs felt weak, I stood and paced to clear my head. My knees buckled when I reached the windowsill. I turned and rested against it. My fingers drummed on the wood on either side.

Agnes shifted uncomfortably in her seat. "We would have to go back and examine the house with magic."

"To make a better plan to go back, we have to go back? That's madness. There has to be a better way. And do we even know if we have to go back? Just because the house is creepy…" I couldn't bring myself to finish the sentence. My fear wanted to keep me as far away from that place as it could. The house had felt wrong on so many different levels. Sometimes, things really were just happenstance. But there were one too many coincidences. I knew instinctively that Meredith's house held answers about our family's curse.

"We should wait for the full moon." Sarah crossed her arms and leaned back in her chair. "At a minimum."

"Wait. Why the full moon?" Grace asked.

Sarah fidgeted under Grace's gaze. "You know how every one of our families is cursed? My curse makes it so I can only access my magic on full moons."

"If we go back in, we should all be able to defend ourselves." Betty stood and stepped next to Sarah. She squeezed her shoulder.

"I could make some protection charms while we wait," Agnes offered.

"Why didn't we have those going in the first time?" I threw up my hands, exasperated.

"They take time." Agnes lowered her head. "And I didn't fully believe there would be something there until we arrived."

I snorted and crossed my arms. The house was creepy last night. She could have mentioned something then.

"What goes into a protection charm?" Grace asked.

Charlie jumped off Grace's lap and sauntered over and rubbed himself against my legs.

"It's a complicated process," Agnes said.

"Can you teach me?" Grace leaned forward and caught Agnes's eye. She gripped the edge of her seat as she stared Agnes down.

"I can—" Agnes began.

"Excellent. Then we should get started. I'm not the fastest student. And the full moon is only, like, a week away," Grace said.

I tried not to gape as Grace bounced in her seat. It was hard to imagine that only a few minutes before, she had been clammy and half conscious. The promise of new lessons seemed to invigorate her.

The Retirees laughed.

"You can follow us back to our place." Betty zipped her coat up. "Agnes is more of a kitchen witch. All of her supplies are there."

Grace scrambled out of her chair as if to follow them out.

"Can I—" My phone chimed in my pocket, interrupting me.

I pulled it out to read the notification. A new claim was waiting in my inbox. I sighed. We had gone to Meredith's house early. It was the beginning of the workday, and I couldn't afford to ignore new claims. Owning my business was expensive. I groaned.

"Maybe next time," I said.

Grace scooped me into a hug. "I promise to take lots of notes."

She released me and scampered after the Retirees as they filtered into the lobby.

I sighed and sat down at my desk to pull open the assignment. As I scanned through the details, my heart sank in my chest—it was a claim for a suicide.

Losing someone was always hard. Claims involving deaths ate at me, and suicides were the worst because the people left behind had so many questions. So much doubt and guilt. The what-ifs worked away at them. Some escaped the guilt, while others were left shell-shocked. And all I could do was tiptoe around them, help with the paperwork, and try to make it a little less difficult.

I reread the assignment directions. The deceased was a

man named Edmund Hastings. He'd lived on the north end of Whidbey Island. And the contact person was his wife's personal assistant. That was a small silver lining. Talking to the family members made such calls especially rough.

I dialed the number on the assignment. A woman answered on the second ring. "This is Patricia Hart."

"Ms. Hart? My name is Dani Williams, with Williams Adjusting."

"You must be with the insurance company. Thank you for calling. The nice lady at our agent's office said you would be reaching out today. I didn't expect it to be so fast." There was a thick quality to her voice, like she had been crying.

"Before we begin, I would like to extend my condolences for your loss. I can't imagine how difficult this must be and understand if you need more time before I come out to... inspect the damages."

She sniffled and blew her nose. "No, no. That's all right. Oh, what do you call them? The biohazard cleanup company? They just arrived. They should be done in about an hour, so if you wanted to come by afterward, that would be good. I've got the family out of the house. Lottie didn't want to leave, but I managed to convince her that a day at the spa would do her some good. I thought it would be best if she didn't have to see you guys."

I took down the rest of the details and hung up. It would take over an hour to get to the north end of the island. Charlie rubbed against my leg then trotted toward the door. "You mind hanging out here for a little while longer?"

Charlie meowed and sat patiently waiting for me to open the door. He darted across the foyer to the insurance agency across the way. It belonged to Olivia, who had taken it over from my grandmother when she passed. She had worked with my gran for so long that she was almost like family. Charlie batted against the door, and before I made it across the shared entryway, Olivia had opened it for him.

Olivia beamed when she saw me standing there. Her hair was up in Bantu knots, and she wore a pink pantsuit. It wasn't a standard color, but she made it look fresh and professional all at the same time. "I thought I heard you come in this morning."

"And I'm about to head back out." I ducked my head toward Charlie. "Mind watching our office mascot for a little while longer?"

"Are you kidding me?" She chuckled. "The day he stops coming over, I'll lose half my foot traffic. I think my clients come in more to see him than they do to see me."

"You're the best," I said.

"Always happy to help." She looked at Charlie as he scampered past her into the office. "I've got a new toy for him, anyway. It's a mouse that rolls away from him. He's going to love it."

I said my goodbyes and retreated to my car. The morning was calm and quiet out on the street. I settled into the front seat and closed my eyes to recenter myself. It had been a roller-coaster ride since I woke up. Quiet morning. Scary encounters. Panic about Grace's reaction to the house. Then back to a quiet morning. My life really had gotten strange ever since I found out I was a witch.

# CHAPTER 3

I rechecked the address on my phone as I pulled up outside the home. *Home* was the wrong word. Estate was more accurate. A tall brick fence faced the street. There was a twelve-foot-tall gate at the entrance to the wide driveway, with a call box built into a brick post in the middle. A camera perched above the entrance. I looked between my phone and the number above the gate. It was the right place.

I turned in to the drive and rolled down my window. I leaned out to press the button. "Hello? This is Dani Williams. I have an appointment with Patricia Hart."

After a few seconds, the gate beeped and swung open. I blinked and slowly rolled through.

Once I was past the gate, the space opened up into a large lawn, with sprawling gardens and a water feature that had been turned off for the winter. The house was a massive plantation-style home with a newer four-car garage off to the side, both painted the same cheery yellow. I pulled to a stop in front of the home and got out.

I grabbed my kit from the trunk. I hadn't made it all the way up the front steps before the massive French doors at the top of them swung open. A middle-aged woman stood in the doorway, her chestnut hair pulled back into a tight bun. She wore a black pencil skirt, sensible heels, and a peach silk blouse that covered her from neck to wrists. I suddenly felt underdressed in my adjuster hoodie and work boots. She blotted her eyes with a tissue as I made my way to her.

"You must be the adjuster." She extended her hand. "I'm Patricia, Mrs. Hastings' assistant."

I shook her hand. "Yes. Dani. Dani Williams. Once again, my condolences for your loss."

Up close, her hazel eyes were red rimmed. There was a puffiness around her nose. She blinked away a tear and took a step back into the home. "I'm glad you could get out so quickly. Like I said on the phone, I've managed to get Lottie out of the house for the day. I didn't think it would do her any good to see this whole process. And the kids—oh God, the kids, they aren't back from school yet."

My heart clenched at the word *kids*. "Do they go nearby?"

"The University of Washington. The youngest just started in the fall. She was moving back into the dorms this week."

I followed Patricia into the house. The home still had so many original wood details, from the crown molding to the elegant filigree carved into the trim around the doors. All the furniture had a sleek, modernist edge, while all of the available surfaces were filled with paintings and sculptures from throughout the ages. The space had an old-meets-new aesthetic, which gave the home a lived-in feel, even though every nook and cranny screamed money and elegance. I trailed Patricia as she led me through the house.

She guided me to an office in the front right corner of the home. The doorframe was cracked where the door had been forced open. She faltered outside the room and steeled herself before pushing it open, her hands shaking. She wiped them on her skirt as she took a quick step back. I peered inside. The cozy room had floor-to-ceiling bookcases lining the walls. A large wooden desk sat in the middle of the room, overlooking the window.

"Lottie found him. She heard the shots. It took over an hour to get in. The police forced it open." Patricia turned away from the room and stared at her hands. "They think when… When he dropped the gun, it went off again. There was a gouge in the floor."

My eyes bounced around the space, quickly taking in the details. There was a bullet hole in the wall on the left. Someone had removed a small section of the wood floor next to the bookcase. My gaze traveled along the floor, which ran parallel to me and entered the hallway. There was no clear break at the door. I kneeled and touched it. *Black walnut?*

"Do you know when the floor was installed?" I asked.

"It's original."

I grabbed my laser measuring tool from my bag and stood. Given the age of the floor, it might be hard to get it to match. Best-case scenario, they would have to sand and refinish the floors for a consistent appearance. "I'm going to have to take some measurements of the hall. Is it continuous into other rooms?"

She nodded.

I started in the hallway and followed her into the dining room, living room, and a sitting room. The kitchen and bathroom had tile, so I didn't need to measure them. With each room, I mentally calculated the size of the claim. I couldn't know for sure, but this one was going to be a doozy. We returned to the office after I had the measurements I needed of the other spaces. Patricia hovered outside the door.

"I think I'm going to go get myself a cup of tea. Do you need anything?" She wrung her hands.

"No, thank you. It should only take me a few more minutes," I said.

She scurried down the hall, and I turned and surveyed the room. My breath came out shaky. I hadn't had a suicide claim since finding out I was a witch. I couldn't tell if the heaviness in the air was from me or from the act that had taken place in the house. Bracing myself, I moved deeper into the room to begin my inspection.

I put my measuring device on the table, and my fingers brushed against a pen on the desk. A flush of adrenaline coursed through me. My heart raced as something cold and heavy settled into my chest. My breath caught in my throat. I swayed in place as the room spun. I crumpled to the ground on my hands and knees, and the cold shifted to warmth. I began to sweat, and my chest constricted. My mind reeled as I tried to make sense of what I was feeling. The emotional residue on the pen and the floor were of shock and confusion. So much confusion. Followed by pain.

After yanking my hand up from the ground, I hugged it to my body as I scrambled to my feet. *Why would he be confused?* I stared at the desk and tried to visualize how he had been sitting based on the missing chair, the direction the desk was facing, and how the various objects were positioned on the desktop. My hands shook as I touched the edge of the desk. Surprise filled me again.

I shook my hand out and slowly touched more and more objects on his desk. Some read as shock, some read as determination, and a few had lingering flashes of joy. Not a single object felt sad or angry. I felt flashes of frustration here and there but barely anything negative at all. *Who kills themselves when they're happy?*

"But the room was locked," I whispered.

I spun in place, my gaze darting around the room for anything, like a piece of art or a photograph, with eyes in it that would have been facing the desk. I knew a spell that would let me look backward in time by accessing the memory of an object, but I could only see the past if the object had physical or metaphorical eyes, like a photo or camera.

There was nothing. No family photos sat on the desk. The artwork on the wall next to the door was a landscape. His computer had a built-in camera, but the lens was covered. There was nothing for me to cast a spell on.

*There has to be something here. Something more concrete.* I paced the room, taking photos as I moved, starting with a picture of the hole in the wall on the left. I quickly scoured his desk, picking up each object and setting it back down. One of the last items I picked up was a pair of scissors. They felt strange in my hand. I turned them over and examined them closely as I opened them. They were left-handed.

I looked back at the hole in the wall. It was on the left. *If he's left-handed and sitting at his desk, wouldn't the hole be on the right?*

Three quick knocks sounded on the door before it cracked open, and Patricia poked her head in.

"Are you almost done?" she asked.

I took a quick photo of the scissors and dropped my camera around my neck. "Yeah. Just need to take a few more measurements." I shifted my laser measuring device on the desk and hit the button for it to diagram the room. "Is it all right if I take a sample of the floor?"

"Go ahead."

"So he was sitting here?" I asked.

She nodded.

"Did the cleaners take the chair?"

She nodded again. "I think they took some photos of it too. I'll get their card so you can ask them about it."

"Thank you." My hands shook as I gathered my things and took a sample of the floor.

I followed her to the foyer to collect the biohazard cleanup company's card. She was sorting the paperwork when the front door slammed open and a young woman strode into the room, overloaded with shopping bags. Her dark-brown hair was piled high on her head in a messy bun, and she wore black harem-style pants, a blue wrap shirt, and an oversized cardigan.

The young woman dropped the bags on the ground and sauntered past us. "Patty, could you get the rest of the bags from my car? I'm too exhausted to bring them all in."

"Of course, Lily." Patty glanced at the bags then out the open front door at the cars in the driveway. "Are the bags for here, or will they be joining you in your dorm room?"

Lily stopped in the archway leading to the hall. She turned and pressed her back into the wall and tossed her head to the side. "I'm not sure. I don't remember everything I bought. Retail therapy is usually a lot more satisfying."

"I'll look through the bags before moving them up to your room, then," Patty said.

Lily nodded. "Thank you. You've always taken such good care of me. I'm going to go take a nap."

Hesitantly, I stepped toward the door.

Lily's head snapped up, and she stared as if noticing me for the first time.

I cleared my throat. "My condolences for your loss."

She nodded again and turned away. She disappeared down the hall, her heels clicking against the wood floor.

Patty coughed and pulled out the biohazard cleanup card from her pile and handed it to me. "Please let me know if you have any other questions."

I took the card and walked in a daze to my car. I stared at the office window at the side of the house. A giant rosebush sat directly in front of the window. It didn't look damaged from there, and someone would have to have climbed right through it to get in or out of that window. *Why was he startled? Did someone kill him? But he was alone. How could someone kill him in a locked room?* I pulled out my phone and called the cleanup company to request the photos. Maybe the images would have answers. My mind was buzzing as I drove down the driveway. *What type of person goes shopping when they hear their dad has died? I guess it's one way to stay busy.*

---

On the entire drive to Point Pleasant, I kept replaying my inspection in my head. It was a locked room. But the emotions I picked up in there didn't make sense for a suicide. *But can I be sure? What does a suicide even feel like?* I wasn't sure I could handle knowing, but during the few conversations I'd had with survivors, they all mentioned feeling hopeless and then at peace once they had made the decision. I imagined the emotions would read similar to that. *Wouldn't they?*

I parked in front of the Bizzy Bean Café. I barely looked up as I made my way to the front door. Normally, the festive window art would bring a smile to my face. Heather had updated it at the start of the year to kittens prancing around, trying to catch snowflakes. Over the past few months, she had been hard at work turning it into a cat café, and her efforts were really paying off.

Inside, it was quiet, well past the midday rush. Heather kept the place open most of the day, with the exception of a couple of hours for lunch and evening cookie prep, for her regulars who liked to camp out at the tables and play with the cats. That day, only a few of the winter interns were gathered along the bar, furiously typing away. With the school year starting again next week, they were trying to finish all their projects before classes began.

Heather wasn't behind the counter. I peeked into the plexiglass cat enclosure. She was in the back corner, waving a feathered cat toy at the end of a stick. Star lay curled on her side on the massive cat tower that took up the left-hand wall, and kittens scampered about, leaping up and down in a desperate attempt to catch the feather.

I slid into the booth across from her and hung my head in

my hands. Heather flipped the feather up again as she turned toward me, a smile on her face. Her expression froze when she saw me.

"I recognize that look," she said.

"What look?" I asked.

"The 'I've encountered something bad and need to talk to someone about it' look."

"Is it that obvious?"

Heather collected the feather toy and tucked it away. The kittens turned on each other and wrestled under our feet.

"So, tell me about it. What happened?"

I slumped forward and rested my forehead against the table. "I just got back from an inspection."

She tapped her fingers, waiting.

I pushed myself up. "The loss notice said it was a suicide."

"Why do I get the feeling there's a *but* coming?" Heather asked.

I tried not to smile. It was a serious conversation, but there was something about Heather that lightened the mood. Or maybe it was the cats. It was hard to be somber with kittens playing under the table.

"But—"

"I knew it." She inched toward me and dropped her voice to a whisper. "A witchy but?"

"Sort of." I shifted in my seat. Heather had been very supportive when she found out I was a witch. I was still getting used to talking about it with other people. At first, it had been just me, but then Betty got added to the list, followed by Grace, Agnes, and Sarah in rapid succession. Heather was the newest addition, although the Retirees didn't know I had told her yet. I fiddled with a napkin as I searched for words. "Something felt off. I touched something on the desk, and... I don't know how to describe it. But it felt like he was startled."

"Do you think he was murdered?"

"Maybe. There were a few other things that didn't really make sense. He was left-handed, but it looks like he was shot on the right. It could be nothing."

"Victor would notice that," Heather said.

"It was near Anacortes. I don't think he would be the medical examiner involved." I sighed and dropped my head into my hands. "Where do I even start? It's in Bob's jurisdiction. I could bring it to Chris, but Bob would have to approve the investigation. And I doubt he would take it seriously coming from me."

"That man really needs to get over himself." Heather snorted. "How long is he going to hold it against you that you solved a murder before him?"

"It's not that." I twisted a napkin between my fingers. "It's Teresa, his wife. After I found out what happened to their son, she lost her battle with cancer. He thinks I took away her will to live."

Heather blew out her breath and collapsed into her seat. "And here I thought it was a pride thing."

I shrugged and tore the napkin in two. There was something oddly therapeutic about ripping up paper.

"Maybe you just need to get back in the room?" Heather asked.

"How? I have no reason to be there. That was my only chance." I closed my eyes. "And I blew it."

"You didn't blow it." Heather squeezed my shoulder. "You're still getting used to this whole witch thing, right? You couldn't have known you were going to stumble across another suspicious death. I mean, what are the chances? Four in six months?"

"Maybe the chances are skewed by what I am." I shrugged. "My heritage is all about divination and fate. Maybe this is my life now. A murder magnet."

"No. Not a murder magnet. You're... a justice seeker. If it wasn't for you, Jessica's killer wouldn't have been brought to justice. Neither would Tina's or Jim's." Heather sat up straight and held my gaze as she spoke. She had a fire in her eyes. "Maybe it is your fate. And that is rough. But it's also important."

I pinched the bridge of my nose and blinked back a tear. It had been rough but also important. And it was too much for me. I needed to focus on my daughter. "I think I'm going to sleep on it and figure out what I'm going to do tomorrow."

I scooted out of the booth, and she walked me to the door. I trudged to my car and drove to my office to pick up Charlie.

Heather knew me too well. She was right. This was important, and I didn't know if I could drop it. One of my first claims had been a fatality. I was there doing my inspection when the husband found out the cause of death was an aneurysm. It didn't make it hurt any less, but at least he wasn't confused anymore. He wasn't blaming himself, thinking he'd missed something. The "if only" went away. It broke my heart every time I handled a claim for a family where the "if only" was all they were left with.

# CHAPTER 4

The entire next day, I tried to focus on the work, but I couldn't get the inspection out of my head. Throughout the day, I had the thought that uncovering murders was now my life. *Did I read the scene right? Was he killed? Why didn't I pick up anything from the killer?* I fidgeted in my seat as I worked on putting together an estimate for the repairs. Every few minutes, I pulled up the photo of the scissors and stared at it. *Would a left-handed person shoot themselves with their right? Maybe there was something wrong with his hand.* I sighed and collapsed into my chair. I stared out the window of my office at Marine View Drive, my eyes focused on the glimpses of the water between the bare trees that lined the roadway.

The minutes ticked away. I hadn't gotten as much done as I would have liked. I glanced at the time on my computer. My date with Chris was in ninety minutes. Every time we tried to do something in Point Pleasant, it ended up getting interrupted by well-meaning busybodies, so we had reserved a spot at a fancy restaurant in Oak Harbor. I chewed on my lip. The restaurant was only fifteen minutes away from the Hastings estate. *Maybe I'll pick something up if I'm nearby.*

When they came, my visions were inconsistent. I couldn't figure out what triggered them, but it wouldn't hurt to try.

I quickly changed into my dress for my date, grabbed my purse, and locked up the office for the day. Because I was heading out for a date straight after work, I hadn't brought Charlie into the office with me. He'd glowered at me as I left that morning. I would have to make sure to take him a treat or I would get the cold shoulder all night when I got home. I wrapped my coat around me and shuffled to the car, my head bent against the wind.

The address for the Hastings estate was still in my GPS from the day before. I selected it and followed the directions out of town. I replayed every second of my inspection in my head as I drove. Edmund Hastings, the victim, had been startled and confused. But not afraid. Not at first, anyway. *Does that mean he knew his killer? You wouldn't be afraid of someone you knew.*

I pulled up across the street from the estate. The brick fence loomed over the road. In the evening light, with murder on my mind, I found the fence foreboding, like it was keeping something in instead of keeping something out. It reminded me of a prison.

After shaking out my arms, I settled into my seat. I closed my eyes and concentrated on the sensations in my body. While I still hadn't fully figured out how to force a vision, I could sometimes get insight based on how my body responded to things. The Sight gave me physical responses to danger or things that were important. There was a heaviness in my chest, but the hairs on my arms were still. I wasn't getting a danger response, but it was clear something was wrong.

My passenger door opened, and I jumped.

I spun in my seat, my heart in my throat. I blinked. A woman I vaguely recognized had climbed into my car next to me. She wore an oversized jacket over a high-waisted pencil skirt that cinched at the waist. Her blue hair hung in waves around her shoulders, with long bangs covering almost half her face. The last time I'd seen her, her hair had been orange. She was the reporter who'd helped me investigate Tina's death. The dark hair made her look a little older than when we last met, but I still couldn't tell if she was in her early, mid, or late twenties. Every part of her face, hair, and wardrobe sent a different message. Her skin and hair were youthful, her clothes fresh and fashionable, but the hunger in her eyes reminded me of the Retirees.

"Izzy?" I asked, my jaw dropping. *What is she doing here?*

"What are you doing here?" she asked, mirroring my thoughts.

"I… Why are you in my car?"

Izzy pushed her hair out of her face and peered at me. "Is this another Tina situation? Are you investigating?"

*Where did she even come from? Why didn't I sense her coming?* I couldn't concentrate on her question. "Another what?"

"Tina situation." Izzy angled her body toward me and studied my face. "Are you the adjuster assigned to the claim? Have you already been in the house? What did you see?"

My mouth opened and closed. I had forgotten how inquisitive she was. But then again, she was a reporter. It made sense. "I am. And I was in there yesterday."

"Then you're back because it's another Tina situation." She grinned and vibrated with excitement. "I knew it."

"I don't know—"

Izzy cut me off with an eye roll. "Oh, come on. You're as curious as I am. We could help each other out."

"How?" I asked.

"You need back in the house, don't you?" Her smile widened. "Or maybe access to the family?"

I nodded.

"I can get you that. I've been assigned to write a memorial

piece. It's not every day that someone like Edmund Hastings passes away. I'll be interviewing the whole family."

"And how do I fit into that?" I asked.

"Well"—she glanced past me at the house—"my usual photographer isn't available. You take pictures, right? If you're interested in some freelance work, you could come along. Keep your eyes open. Maybe suggest a question or two along the way."

The pressure at the back of my head was building. The opportunity was one I couldn't pass up, but it sounded too good to be true. "And what do you get out of it?"

"I would be helping you on one condition. If you find something, you tell me about it. If this is a Tina situation, if he was murdered, that would take this from a midpaper story to front-page news. And not just in the *Island County Gazette*. I might be able to get it into King 5 or... even something national."

I blanched at the thought of my name connected to something national in scope. Bob, the local sheriff, already didn't like me. I didn't want that dislike to evolve into outright loathing.

"You would, of course, remain completely anonymous." She held my gaze. "If that's what you want."

"Completely anonymous? You promise?"

"I do." She held out her hand.

I eyed it.

"On my career."

I reached out and shook her hand.

She leaned back, a satisfied smile on her face, and rummaged in her bag. She pulled out a notebook and scrawled something on it before ripping out the page and handing it to me. "Our first interview is in the morning at ten a.m. See you then."

Izzy flung open the passenger door and climbed out. She strode away and got into a car parked behind me. I stared at the note. It was a name and an address. Nicholas Hastings. The interview would happen at his workplace, Hastings Timber.

I had an in, but I couldn't help but wonder if I had just made a deal with the devil. Izzy had been helpful last time. But it was hard not to feel uneasy when your partner was doing it just to get ahead.

I glanced at the clock on my dash—6:43 p.m. My date with Chris was quickly approaching. I didn't have time to sit and think about Izzy's offer. I shoved the note into my coat pocket, put my car in Drive, and followed my GPS to Oak Harbor.

The restaurant was in a two-story building that reminded me of homes in the area. Split levels were all over the Seattle region, more so than in any other area I had lived in. The restaurant had a porch that wrapped around the front with a classy sign built into the railing. Chris and I had shared a few kisses, but our attempts to go on a date had been thwarted until then. I swallowed hard as I fixed my hair in the car mirror. *What if he changes his mind? What if this turns out like Ed, where he liked the* idea *of me more than the real me?*

I pushed the negative self-talk aside and got out of the car. With the sun down, the temperature had dropped a few degrees. We were close enough to the water that it never got too cold. Even at that time of year, it rarely dropped below freezing. But the humidity always made it feel colder. I pulled my coat around me and strode toward the restaurant.

My breath caught in my throat as I pushed open the front door. The restaurant was fancier than any place I had been, at least recently. My heels clicked against the hardwood floors. They were a warm cherry that made the space feel inviting. Track lighting hidden inside the crown molding set the mood. The place oozed romance.

Chris had beaten me there. He sat at a booth by the window, and he stood as I entered. He wore a black suit jacket over black jeans and a black button-up shirt. The top button was undone, revealing the top of his collarbone. He stared at me, starry-eyed, with a grin plastered over his face. We had both dressed up for the occasion. He hadn't seen me in a dress since high school, but I still tidied up well after all those years. I wore a red wrap dress that flowed around my legs and accentuated my curves.

He didn't stop smiling as I sashayed across the room. I didn't look around. I just held his gaze. My heart skipped a beat as I drew closer. He looked happier to see me than Ed ever had, even on our wedding day.

"You cleaned up nice," I said.

He drew me into a hug and kissed the top of my head. "You look amazing. I feel like I'm the luckiest guy in the world."

I pulled away a few inches, my fingers still lingering on his arms. "You're setting that bar awfully high for me."

He pushed a stray lock of hair behind my ear. "I've known you long enough to know you'll meet it."

I ducked, blushing, and slid into the booth. He took a seat opposite me.

It was hard not to stare. Most of the time I saw Chris, he was either in his deputy uniform or wearing flannels. It was almost hard to believe we had officially entered the girl-friend-boyfriend phase of our relationship. *I'm forty. Not a teenager. Get ahold of yourself!* I bit the inside of my lip and picked up the menu.

"Have you been here before?" I asked.

"No." He ran his hand through his hair, a sheepish smile on his face. "I haven't really dated in a few years. And this always seemed like a special-occasion type place. How about you?"

"Same."

It was a short menu with only a few starters and entrees. Reading the descriptions made my mouth water. After a few minutes of back-and-forth banter, we settled on the pistachio-crusted rack of lamb over garlic mashed potatoes for Chris, and scallops over a vegetable risotto for me. After ordering, we sat and stared at each other. I hadn't been on a date since before Grace was born. *What am I supposed to say?*

Chris cleared his throat. "How was your day?"

"Slow. It's that awkward time at the beginning of the year when not many claims are submitted. It'll pick back up here soon."

"Does that mean you'll have more free time?" he asked.

"Maybe." I fiddled with my napkin. "I may have just agreed to do some freelance photography work."

"That's great." He squeezed my hand. "Your landscape photos are beautiful."

"It would be a bit different than that."

"Oh?" He raised an eyebrow.

"It's probably going to be family photos. Or... funeral photos?" I squirmed in my seat. Chris knew me too well. After spilling that detail, I would have to tell him more about the project.

He chuckled and shook his head. "Why am I not surprised? You always seem to get caught up in morbid stuff. Whose funeral?"

"Edmund Hastings's. I inspected his house yesterday." I pursed my lips. "Something didn't feel right."

"And you want to get closer so you can investigate it?"

Our waiter arrived with our food. I paused while he backed away from the table before I responded.

"I don't know. Maybe." I pushed my scallops around my plate with my fork, trying to figure out what to say next. "What do you think I should do?"

"Keep me in the loop."

I choked on my bite of food. That wasn't the response I was expecting. "So you're okay with me investigating again?"

"Your instincts haven't led you wrong yet." He took a bite

of his lamb and chewed thoughtfully. "I'm not happy about you potentially putting yourself in danger again. But I can't expect you to be someone you're not and have this work. I have to accept that you investigate dangerous things. And you have to accept that I'll always worry. So, keep me in the loop."

I stood and leaned over the table, careful not to drag my dress through the food. I kissed him. "You are a good man, Deputy Harris."

We spent the rest of the meal talking. He told me about his decision to get into law enforcement and his one failed relationship after college. We both had a passion for justice, and he wanted to help the community. I told him what it was like raising Grace and how scary it was now that she was practically an adult. It was comfortable.

After dinner, we strolled two blocks down to the harbor and sat on top of a covered picnic table as we stared out at the water. He wrapped his arm around my shoulders, and I nestled into his side, my head resting on his chest.

After months of failed starts, we had finally had our first proper date. And it was perfect.

# CHAPTER 5

The first interview was in Mount Vernon at the Hastings Timber headquarters. I took the ferry into Mukilteo and followed my GPS. That far north of Seattle, it didn't take much to feel like I was in the middle of nowhere. Cities gave way to farmland. Something about the hills coming off the cascade mountains created the illusion of solitude. Towns quickly disappeared over the crest of the hills. The only thing that kept the area feeling populated was the other cars on the highway.

I pulled up in front of the building. Steel siding gleamed under the midmorning sun. The front of the structure had been gutted and replaced with floor-to-ceiling windows filled with reflective glass. The exterior finishes were at odds with the shape of the building, giving it a recently refurbished look. I parked and grabbed from the passenger seat a box of cookies that I had picked up at the Bizzy Bean. With the box tucked under one arm and my camera case slung over the other shoulder, I strode toward the building.

Izzy stood waiting for me outside the front door. Her blue hair sat snug against her head in a French braid. She hugged her plaid peacoat to her body while stamping her feet against the ground for warmth.

"For a minute, I was worried you weren't going to come." Izzy held the door open for me.

"And miss out on the important questions? Never." I forced cheer into my voice. My hands were clammy. I had been taking photos for years, but the current assignment was something new. *What if I can't take good enough photos? She'll have to hire someone else. This might be my only shot.*

I stepped inside. Almost everything was crafted of wood. Wooden floors. Wooden desks. Wood paneling along the lower section of the walls. In most other places, that much wood would have been overpowering. But each section had been carefully selected so that the different colors and grains complemented each other. It made sense. Wood was their business.

I followed Izzy to the receptionist's desk. A young woman sat behind the massive counter that had been carved out of a single piece of wood. She wore a green polo shirt with the company's logo stitched onto the breast. She looked up from her cell phone as we approached. Her eyes bounced from Izzy to me and back again. She landed on me and smiled. "You must be Ms. Carter."

Izzy stepped forward and thrust her hand out. "Nope. That would be me. Isabel Carter. Although most people call me Izzy."

The girl blinked.

"Is Mr. Hastings ready for us?" Izzy asked, pulling her hand back.

The girl fumbled with her mouse as she checked his schedule. "It looks like he's still on a call. He should be available in a few more minutes. I'll let you know when he's ready."

Izzy nodded and stepped away from the counter.

My heart raced. *What if—Oh, shut up. I've got this. Check the lighting. Take a few test shots. I brought two cameras so I can play with film versus digital. Stop doubting yourself.* The pep talk didn't help. My mouth was dry, and I struggled to swallow.

"Could I bother you for a glass of water?" I asked.

"Of course." The girl stood and walked around the desk. "Follow me. We have some spare mugs in the breakroom."

I left Izzy waiting in the lobby. The wood theme continued down the hall and into the breakroom. Instead of plastic chairs, wooden stools with plush cushions were scattered around tables. I trailed the receptionist as she grabbed a glass from the cupboard, opened the fridge, and retrieved a pitcher of water. I peeked over her shoulder as she opened the door. Leftover sheet cake took up half the fridge.

"That thing is massive," I said.

She laughed and handed me the glass. "We've been eating cake for days. I'm going to have to throw it out soon."

I sipped the cool water. That, combined with her relaxed demeanor, helped quiet my anxiety. "What was it for? A retirement or something?"

"Nick's promotion." She rested her hip against the counter. "He's the new chief administrative officer."

My eyes widened, and I took another sip. "I hadn't heard."

She glanced over my shoulder. "His meeting should be wrapping up right around now."

I followed her to her desk. While she checked his schedule again, I scurried over to Izzy. I leaned in close and whispered, "Guess who just got a promotion?"

Her expression froze. "Nick?"

I nodded. "CAO."

"He's ready to see you now," the girl said.

I pulled back from Izzy and followed the two of them through the building. We took the elevator up to the third floor. Nick's office was at the rear of the building, overlooking Mount Baker. My eyes bounced from the breathtaking view to the man behind an impressive oak desk.

Nicholas Hastings stood when we entered the room. He was well over six feet tall, and his shoulders were broad. He wore a gray button-up shirt over blue jeans. It looked like he couldn't have been more than a few years out of college. He was young, maybe twenty-five or twenty-six. I met his steel-blue eyes and swallowed. While he had an outwardly young appearance, his eyes told a different story. There was a seriousness in them that came only with experience.

Izzy strode across the room and shook his hand. "Thank you for taking time to speak with me. I'm Izzy." She gestured over her shoulder at me. "And this is my associate, Dani Williams. She'll be taking a few photographs while we talk."

He nodded and motioned for her to sit.

"I just wanted to start off by extending my condolences. I know talking about your father at a time like this must be difficult, so if you need to take any breaks while we talk, please let me know."

"I don't have a lot of time today, so let's get this taken care of. What's your first question?" Nick asked, impatience creeping into his voice.

I shuffled around the room, checking the lighting. Over the years, I'd learned how to actively listen while working. Listening was a real skill. It wasn't just about being quiet while someone talked; it was about understanding and creating a rapport. I held my tongue and let Izzy take the lead. I didn't envy her having to get Nicholas Hastings to open up. His tone was borderline hostile.

"It always amazes me how someone can have so many different sides to them." Izzy perched on the edge of her seat, notebook at the ready. "I'm hoping to capture as many sides of your father as I can. So, who was Edmund Hastings to you? What type of man was he?"

"A father. A mentor. He took the lumber business seriously and expected the same from me. I learned almost *everything* I know from him." His voice was even, and there was something practiced, almost rehearsed, about the way he spoke and moved.

"Do you have any memories of him that stand out more than others?"

"Like, what was our happiest moment together?"

"If that's what sticks out most to you." Izzy crossed her legs and studied him over the edge of her notebook.

I hid a smile. Her technique was good—open-ended questions. She was guiding the conversation without forcing it in any particular direction. She would have been a good adjuster.

Hastings continued. "A camping trip when I was eleven. We went down to California to the redwood forest. It was awe-inspiring to be surrounded by so much old growth. We have some amazing forests up here but nothing quite that grand."

I crouched next to his desk and set up my tripod. While he wasn't looking, I reached out to touch the edge of his desk. He was touching the corner of the desk with his knee. I didn't have the skill Grace did to pick up emotions from people, but I had discovered a work-around. If I touched something someone else was touching, I could pick up things in real time. Sometimes.

My muscles tensed as my breath caught in my throat. My stomach became tight. *What does this mean?* I lowered my head over my camera and closed my eyes. *Concentrate. Why can't I be as good at this as my daughter? What is this feeling? Caution?*

"So the trees are what tied you together?"

"You could say that." Nick shrugged and readjusted.

I cursed under my breath as he stopped touching the desk.

"How did he feel about your recent promotion?" Izzy asked.

"It's been in the works for a while. I think the excitement

of it all wore off when we agreed to the transition six months ago." He checked his watch. "The title change was largely a formality at this point."

I pursed my lips as I checked the lighting again. *He's too guarded to give honest answers.* I glanced at the box of cookies I had carried in with me. A relaxation spell could be helpful.

"I think the lighting is good here," I cut in. "Oh, I almost forgot. I stopped by the bakery on my way in and picked up some cookies. Would you like one?" I opened the box and offered Izzy a cookie. She took it. I turned to Nick.

He shook his head. "I have a food tasting coming up in an hour for my wedding. I am not prepared to withstand the wrath of my fiancée if I ruin my appetite before getting there."

I took a seat next to Izzy and tried to hide my disappointment.

Izzy took a bite of her cookie and set it on the arm of her chair. "Congratulations on your coming wedding."

"Thank you." He settled back in his chair and crossed his hands over his stomach. "We weren't sure if we should reschedule or not. We've had our venue booked for almost a year. I think it'll feel strange either way. Is there anything else you need?"

"We're almost done." Izzy glanced at me. I shrugged, and she continued. "Does your father's death change much? I understand he was still the CEO."

"On a personal level, of course. He was my father. He'll be missed. On a business level? Not much. It moves timetables forward on the paperwork side, but the day-to-day operations will be the same. Hastings Timber has been in the family for generations, and I'm sure it will continue long after I'm gone as well." He glanced at his watch again. "I should hit the road soon if I don't want to be late for the tasting. How long will the photos take?"

I jumped up and finished readying my equipment. "Only

a few minutes, although I would like to get a few shots of the lumberyard out back as well."

He nodded and shifted in his seat.

I focused on his face. Day-old stubble covered his chin. His brown hair was lightly tousled. I directed him to move a little to the left then snapped a few photos.

After I finished up in the yard, I returned to my car. Izzy was waiting for me. She stood hugging her coat to her and staring at her shoes.

"What do you think?" she asked.

"He was hard to read. He didn't seem... sad. But if all they had in common was work, maybe they weren't that close."

She nodded and pursed her lips. "Okay. The middle child is next. His name is Sebastian. He attends U-Dub. Our interview is at eight p.m." She handed me a slip of paper with his address. "See you there."

She strode to her car and slipped inside. I took a seat in my car and watched her drive away. Nicholas had been hard to read. *Was he cautious because he has something to hide or because she's a reporter?* I pulled out my notepad and wrote down his name. I put a question mark next to it.

He was the first suspect on my list, but I didn't feel certain he should be there.

# CHAPTER 6

For the entire drive back to Point Pleasant, I replayed the interview in my head. Izzy had asked good questions, but I was frustrated at not being able to lead myself, although I might not have been able to get much more out of Nick myself. He was a closed book. He kept his responses short and succinct. It wasn't that his answers left me with more questions but that they left me with no threads to pull. Nicholas Hastings was an enigma, just like his dad.

I parked in front of the Bizzy Bean and darted through the front door as Heather flipped the sign from Open to Closed. She always closed up shop from two to four to have lunch and get a jump start on baking for the evening rush.

"You mind if I join you for lunch?" I asked.

"I'm out of leftovers, so if you don't mind eating out." She grabbed her coat from behind the counter.

I followed her out onto the street. "Oh no. Twist my arm. Not out to eat."

She chuckled and locked the front door behind us. We strolled the few blocks to Abby's bistro, Eats and Treats. That time of day, it was mostly empty. The lunch rush had ended, and only a few stragglers remained.

"Your usual?" Abby looked up from behind the counter. She had recently chopped off most of her hair into a pixie cut.

Heather nodded, and we took a seat at the back. I gave Heather a quizzical look as we sat down. Abby's menu changed weekly.

Heather shrugged. "My response is to surprise me. She hasn't picked wrong yet."

I grinned. Abby did have a way of choosing the best options. Once someone became a regular, she got a feel for what they liked. She hadn't served me wrong yet, either.

"I've decided to investigate," I said.

Heather tensed and opened her mouth.

I held up my hand. "And before you say anything, I promise to keep you updated and to have a buddy with me whenever I do anything dangerous."

"A buddy?" She cocked an eyebrow.

"I... may have an unusual *in* for my investigation." I intertwined my fingers in front of me and tapped my thumbs together. "Do you remember Isabel Carter?"

"The reporter?"

"She's writing the memorial piece for the *Island County Gazette*. She's hired me to take photos."

Heather relaxed into the booth. "Does she... know?"

I shook my head. "You're the only non-witch I've told."

Abby dropped our food off at our table. She hovered for a second and watched us take our first bites. We were still in the heart of winter, so soup dominated Abby's menu. She served a white bean soup to Heather and a cabbage beef stew to me. Each soup had a giant slice of cheesy garlic bread on the side. I stifled a groan as I bit into a piece of beef. It was perfectly tender and melted in my mouth.

Heather broke off a piece of her bread. "Delicious."

Abby bounced on the balls of her feet and sauntered to the counter.

"What's the plan?" Heather broke off another piece of bread.

I pulled out the interview schedule. While I didn't have all the locations yet, I had the times. "We interviewed the oldest son this morning. The middle child is tonight, and it looks like we're interviewing the daughter tomorrow. The interview for the wife hasn't been scheduled yet."

"Did the oldest give you any leads?"

"Not really." I filled her in on the interview.

She ate her soup thoughtfully. "It might help if you knew a bit more about them before the interviews. Have you looked them up yet?"

I shook my head and pulled out my phone. She grabbed hers, and we sat hunched over our tiny screens, searching for what information we could find about them online.

We split the list. Heather started with Nick, and I started with Sebastian. Nick was on all the standard sites I would have expected for a young, working professional. He had a fair amount of public-facing posts and photos, but they were well curated. Everything was professional and polished. Much like the interview, he didn't leave any dangling threads to pull on. Sebastian—or Bash to his friends—was a very different story. There was photo after photo of him drinking and partying. He was definitely the wild child of the group.

"Maybe Bash was going to get cut out of the will. He doesn't look like he got along with his family much," I said. "Although, if that's the case, I'm surprised they let us schedule an interview with him."

Heather shrugged. "Maybe less was expected? There's usually more pressure on the eldest."

We moved on to the other family members. Heather grunted, clearly frustrated as she repeatedly encountered private settings on daughter Lily's pages. All we could tell was that she was involved in theater, and that was the end of it. There wasn't a single public photo, outside of publicity shots for plays she was performing in, that was newer than two years old. Charlotte's page was also relatively private. Her few public-facing posts had the same professional look as those of her eldest sons. I scrolled through a few pages, reading through Hastings Timber announcements, and paused over a two-month-old article.

Charlotte Hastings had been the CFO of Hastings Timber until a month ago, when she was replaced by someone outside the family.

I passed my phone to Heather, and she read the article. She buzzed with excitement. "Trouble in paradise, maybe? That's a lot of changes. There's not a single quote from Charlotte in here. If she was happy about the transition, she would have said something, right?"

I braced my forearms on the table, a smile spreading wide across my face. "Exactly. And she's the one who found the body."

"Looks like you've found your prime suspect. And I may have found a few more people worth talking to." Heather put my phone on the table then slid hers across. "Live-in staff. A personal chef and gardener. If there was trouble in paradise, the help always knows."

"That's brilliant." I jotted down the names.

"Now you just have to get them added to the interview list."

I sucked my lower lip between my teeth. "I don't have control over the interview list."

"Izzy's a smart girl." Heather nudged my phone toward me. "It doesn't hurt to ask."

> **DANI**
> Have you thought about interviewing the household staff?

> **IZZY**
> Patricia?

> **DANI**
> And the chef. Or the gardener.

**IZZY**
Names?

> **DANI**
> Matteo Patel and Penelope Cooper.

**IZZY**
Adding them now.

We relaxed into the booth. I picked up the last piece of garlic bread and tore it in half. I chewed on a piece as I contemplated my next move. It was odd having to do things in tandem with someone else. But Izzy was my in, and I didn't have a choice. Not really.

We finished eating our lunch. Heather hopped out of the booth and said her farewells before heading to the café to bake a batch of cookies for her evening rush. I followed her out and made my way to my car. I had taken both digital and film shots. The film wasn't strictly necessary, but it made it more fun. I headed home to develop the film in my darkroom before the next interview.

# CHAPTER 7

For the second time that day, I took the ferry across to Mukilteo. It was late enough in the afternoon that most of the rush hour congestion had cleared up. But traffic headed into Seattle was never good. There was always a bottleneck where the HOV lane ended and the express lanes began. At that time of day, it was closed, and all the carpoolers were darting over well before the lane ended. I took the exit for the university and wound my way through the packed downtown.

The University of Washington was a sprawling campus that had its own ecosystem built up around it. I parked in one of its underground parking garages and walked the four blocks to Bash's apartment just off campus. Izzy was waiting for me outside, and we took the elevator up to his floor. He had a corner unit that overlooked the street. Music was playing loudly inside. Izzy knocked twice before he answered.

Bash was even taller than his brother, Nick. Ducking to avoid hitting the doorframe, he peered out into the hall. He had the same chestnut-brown hair, but it was unruly and fell in haphazard waves around his face. He also had the same piercing blue eyes, although instead of looking serious, they had an edge of mischief. He looked Izzy up and down.

"Are you that reporter Patricia's making me talk to?"

Izzy didn't miss a beat. She thrust out her hand and plastered a smile onto her face. "Isabel Carter. You can call me Izzy."

Her hand disappeared into his as he shook it. His smile widened, and he stepped back into his apartment.

We followed him into a spacious living room. A large leather couch sat in the middle of the room, facing a massive eighty-inch TV on the far wall. Movie posters lined the walls. There was something cohesive about the decor that made it all feel like it belonged to one person.

"And you are?" he asked.

"Dani." I lifted my bag. "The photographer."

"That's dope." He flopped down on the couch.

Izzy pulled a barstool from the kitchen counter and perched on top of it. I hovered nearby, unpacking my bag and listening in.

"Before we get started, I wanted to extend my condolences for your loss. I know interviews like this, especially when everything is still so fresh, can be difficult. If you need to take a break, please let me know." Izzy pulled out her notebook.

"The boys took me on a wallowing bar hop last night. I think I've got most of the grief out of my system." His gaze flicked to her legs. "Although if you wanted to go back out, I'm sure I could rustle up another good cry."

I turned my back. I couldn't hide my wide-eyed expression. *Wallowing bar hop? Who does that?*

Izzy cleared her throat and continued, ignoring his suggestion. "Could you tell me about your father? What type of man was he?"

"I don't know. Seriously? I don't think he ever took a vacation or loosened up a day in his life." He grabbed a ball from the side table and threw it up into the air and caught it. "He loved wood."

*Is he going to say anything useful?* I peered down the hallway and glanced back at him. From the angle he was sitting, he wouldn't be able to see me if I went down the hall. Snooping might be a better use of my time.

"Do you have a restroom I could use?" I cut in before Izzy could ask a follow-up question.

"Sure thing." He tossed the ball into the air. "Second door on the right."

I nodded and wandered into the hall. I carefully opened the first door. It led to a home gym. There was an impressive array of weights and equipment for one guy. I closed the door and continued down the hall. It was a three-bedroom place. The first room was the gym, the second was a bedroom, and the third was an office. I paused there. *Why would he need an office?*

I glanced down the hall. The voices were muffled by the distance. Izzy was in the middle of her "tell me your most vivid memory" question. I darted into the office. I didn't have long. And something about the office felt off. A desk took up the right-hand wall. Two bookcases stood on the other side and a printer station on the far-left wall. The art in the room differed from that in the rest of the house. A beautiful land-scape next to the door reminded me of the Hastings estate. The spines of the books were slightly cracked, as if they had been opened many times. I kneeled in front of the bookshelf and read the titles—an odd mix of poetry, pre-law textbooks, and books on environmental sciences.

I touched the textbook. The hair on the back of my neck rose. I clenched my jaw. *Determination? Curiosity?* My fingers lingered over books of poetry. Butterflies took flight in my stomach. My head felt light. *Joy?* I stood. The room was full of contradictions. That room belonged to an intellectual, and Bash didn't strike me as one.

I stepped up to the desk and pulled open the drawers. The bottom drawer was filled with notebooks, and I quickly thumbed through them. Page after page was filled with notes written in big blocky letters. They were for environmental science classes. I couldn't make heads or tails of them. I slid them back into place and continued up to the next drawer, which was filled with graded papers. They had Sebastian's name on them, and he was apparently doing well in school. I flipped to another page. Very well. Almost every paper had an A in red at the top.

I glanced at the door. I couldn't linger for much longer, so I quickly snapped a photo of his textbook collection and the top page of his latest assignment and ducked into the hall. I padded to the bathroom and slipped inside. Even that room was tidy, but it still had a bachelor feel with a single toothbrush and bar soap in the shower. I flushed the toilet then flipped through the photos on my phone as I ran the water. *Who are you? Playboy jock or serious student?* I turned the water off and walked into the hall. Bash seemed like another family member with a carefully constructed image. *Will any of these interviews be useful?*

I wandered into the living room. Izzy was jotting down notes from his last answer.

Bash flung the ball up into the air. "Honestly, this whole thing just confuses me."

Izzy's pen froze over her notebook. She looked up at him. "How so?"

"I mean, it's not like we've been close. Not in a few years." He caught the ball and threw it right back up. "I am The Great Disappointment, after all."

"Did you think Patricia would leave you off the interview list?" she asked.

He shook his head and sat up. The ball landed next to him on the couch. It bounced and rolled away across the room. "No. Him being gone. It's probably why it hasn't fully hit me yet. It doesn't feel real. He was always uptight. He lived and breathed stress. But... he was a completionist. Does that make sense? He never did anything halfway."

I stepped into the room and kneeled by my bag to finish setting up the camera. There was that familiar pressure at the back of my head that appeared almost every time something important was about to be said. I moved slowly so I wouldn't interrupt his thought process. Izzy apparently had a similar idea. She sat stock-still on the stool, waiting for him to finish.

He gripped the edge of the couch, his shoulders rounding. He stared at his feet. There was an intensity in his eyes, and grief bubbled under the surface. But it didn't overflow. His next words had that same boyish tone that he'd had for the rest of the conversation. "I guess I thought if he was going to do it, he would have waited until after he finished changing his will. It just seems so out of character to leave something undone."

"What will change?" I blurted out.

He blinked and shook his head. He turned toward me and held my gaze. "I thought everyone knew. He was changing things up. Our whole lives, we were going to get an even split, everything doled out evenly among his children. But he was shifting things around and specifying what each one of us was going to inherit."

"Does that mean... you would get less?" I asked.

He shrugged. "Technically. But it's so much, who cares? I'm not looking forward to dealing with my part of the company. I would have preferred the real estate he was going to leave me."

"So, who was going to get the company?" I asked as I fiddled with my camera settings.

"Nick. I was getting some real estate. Mom was getting the house and money. And Lily was getting his entire art collection. At least, that's what he told me. It's not like I ever saw the will." He stood and stretched. "So, where do you want me for the photos?"

I directed him to a chair in the corner. I set up the lights around him and took a few shots. While I was shooting, he went back to his playful self and tried to convince Izzy to grab a drink with him. She ended up giving him her card and politely saying maybe later.

After I took the last of the photos, I followed Izzy down the elevator. We stood in front of the building, hugging our coats to ourselves.

"Did you find anything useful?" she asked.

"He's a pre-law, environmental sciences student."

She rocked back on her heels. "Huh. I can't say I saw that coming. He didn't seem the type."

"Maybe he's the black sheep of the family for more than one reason." I fidgeted with my coat. "But I don't know. He seemed genuinely bummed that the will change hadn't gone through."

"Agreed." She pursed her lips. "There has to be someone who is happy about it, though. And whoever that is, is going to be our prime suspect."

# CHAPTER 8

When I pulled into the driveway of my home, two vehicles were already parked outside—Grace's car and Betty's truck. I pulled halfway onto the frozen grass so I wouldn't block them in. I trudged up the front steps and found the group inside, gathered around the kitchen table. Betty and Sarah sat to one side, mortar and pestle in hand, grinding herbs. Grace sat hunched over her notebook, frantically writing directions as Agnes ticked off the various steps of the spell. Charlie lay sprawled behind them on his cat perch, his eyes closed and his one paw jutting out to touch Grace on her shoulder.

"Is it too late for me to jump in on the lesson?" I asked.

Grace tilted her head up and glanced at me before returning to her writing. "I've been taking notes for the both of us."

I shrugged off my coat and hung it up in the closet. "Where do I begin?"

Betty thrust a third mortar and pestle into my hands. "Help us prep the ingredients."

I peered into the bowl. *Rosemary?* I cocked an eyebrow and ground the fresh leaves. "So, what are we making?"

"A few things." Grace looked up from her notebook again.

Agnes nodded and paused in her directions.

"Protective amulets"—Grace ticked things off on her fingers—"protective tinctures, a cleansing tincture, and a cleansing incense."

My eyes widened. "Why so many?"

"They all do different things." Grace glanced at Agnes again before continuing. "The protective amulets we're making can help shield the wearer from psychic attacks. But they only work while being worn. The protective tincture gives an added layer of protection, but it doesn't last long, so it's something you would drink before going into a dangerous situation. The cleansing tincture is in case something still sneaks through, and the cleansing incense might help make the house feel less... creepy."

"You're a good student." Agnes beamed.

"Not really." Grace blushed. "You're just an excellent teacher."

Agnes blushed, too, and shifted in her seat. She fiddled with a set of black stones arrayed in front of her. "I wouldn't go that far. Protective magic isn't my specialty. There's no guarantee any of this is going to work as well as I would like. Hence all the redundancies. If I was really good at protective magic, we would just need the amulets."

"What are your specialties?" I took a seat at the table and glanced from Agnes to Sarah. Betty told me hers. Her specialty was the power of change, known as transmutation.

"Illusion," Agnes said.

Sarah added more herbs to her mix. "Evocation."

"What's that?" Grace asked.

"Control over the elements." Sarah tamped down the pile with the pestle. "I can move rocks around. Create windstorms. Turn water into ice. Or light things on fire."

Grace's jaw dropped. "Wow. That's so cool." She leaned back, her expression pensive. "But you can only do that on the full moon, right?"

Sarah nodded.

Grace gestured toward Betty. "And something always goes wrong with your spells. That's why you're not taking the lead on this."

"That's right."

"And we have no control over our visions. Then what's your curse?" Grace asked, looking at Agnes.

The table went quiet. Betty stood and wrapped her arms around Agnes.

Agnes buried her head into Betty's shoulder. "I can never leave Point Pleasant."

"What?" I blurted. My jaw dropped.

"We didn't know at first," Betty began. "When we were kids, we used to dream about traveling."

"We worked odd jobs and saved up." Sarah stood and put her hand on Agnes's shoulder. "Our first summer after high school, we jumped in a car and tried to go on a road trip."

"My mom believed that our family had been spared somehow," Agnes said as she peered at me over Betty's shoulder. "I was the first to try to leave, you see."

"It started with an upset stomach," Betty said.

"We thought she was carsick," Sarah continued. "But then a fever set in."

"We hadn't even made it to Olympia when she lost consciousness." Betty blinked back a tear.

I covered my mouth, my gaze flicking from Betty to Agnes to Sarah. They had always been there. It had never crossed my mind that they couldn't leave.

"Mel is the one who figured it out." Agnes squeezed Betty's hand. "And we hightailed it back home."

"The second we crossed the boundary back into town, she was fine." Sarah rubbed Agnes's shoulder.

"And this is where we've stayed ever since," Agnes said. "I've trapped them here."

"No." Betty shook her head. "Everyone has dreams of

what their life is going to be like when they're young. And living a different life doesn't mean that it wasn't worth living."

"And for me, it stayed the same in all the important ways," Sarah said. "I dreamed of living with my best friends. I couldn't leave either one of you behind."

"Same." Betty nodded. "I dreamed of growing old with my partner in crime. We've succeeded at the important parts."

"I love it here," Sarah said. "Staying in one spot lets us build a community. We couldn't have done that as well on the road."

"You guys." Agnes pulled Sarah and Betty into a hug. "I couldn't be stuck here with better people."

Grace caught my eye. We stared at each other over the table. Her expression mirrored my own. Our mouths were pinched, and our eyes were hard. It wasn't just about Grace getting a good night's sleep anymore. Point Pleasant had become a prison for Agnes. A very nice, comfortable prison, but that didn't change the facts. Some of my favorite memories were of a camping trip at Priest Lake and a road trip through the Rainbow Mountains in Utah. It wasn't too late for Agnes to have that too. And we were going to make it happen for her.

Sarah and Betty returned to their seats and began grinding their herbs once more.

"All right. We're almost done with the prep work. Next step is to cast the spells together."

"Together? Like at the same time?" I asked.

"More than just at the same time." Agnes straightened. "It's a melding of our energies."

"It's why witches gather in covens," Betty said. "You didn't think it was just for the company, did you?"

"I… I hadn't thought about it." I blinked.

"Witches are stronger when they work together," Sarah

said. "It's like… making rope. Braiding it makes it stronger than the sum of its parts."

Agnes handed Grace and me pieces of paper with the words of a spell written on them. "Let's practice saying it together first. Once we've got that down, we'll try casting the spell together. It works best if we link hands. You'll want to visualize handing the strands of your magic to me, and I'll take it from there."

After our third failed attempt to say the words at the same time, Sarah came up with the idea of putting them to music. We all knew the tune for "Rudolph the Red-Nosed Reindeer," so we decided to use that. It was awkward at first, a jumble of nonsensical sounds, but we eventually synced up perfectly. It took only seven more attempts. Sarah clapped the beat to keep us synced. While she couldn't cast magic without the full moon, she still wanted to help.

I followed Agnes's directions and linked hands with them. Agnes's hand was warm from all her hand-wringing. Betty's hand was cool and dry to the touch. Agnes started the chant. I stared wide-eyed as light gathered around her. Her lights had an iridescent quality. The colors shifted between purple, green, and teal. It was breathtaking to watch. Grace picked up after her, adding her purple sparkles to the mix.

We went around the table, each witch joining in one after the other. Betty's lights were oddly shaped, almost pearl-like globes that floated around us. Finally, it was my turn. I joined the chant. My motes of light danced between us. I furrowed my brow and concentrated. *Go to Agnes.* My lights swirled through the air and settled around Agnes. The lights from all the other witches followed suit until Agnes was bathed in a swarm of flickering lights. She glowed brightly as she chanted the last words of the spell. The light coalesced into five balls, which slowly drifted down to the black rocks on the table and settled into the stones. The black surfaces twinkled for a second then were still.

I sat slack-jawed, staring at the stones. "That was beautiful."

Agnes picked up the stones and handed them out. "These are black tourmalines. You'll want to wrap them with wire or put them in a bag to wear around your neck."

I nodded. My hand closed around the stone. It was still warm. I could feel the energy buzzing under the surface.

"All right. One down, three more to go," Betty said, handing out scraps of paper with the words to the next spell written on them. It was going to be a long night.

# CHAPTER 9

We successfully made the protective and cleansing charms and tinctures. We finished around midnight. The spells were complicated, and I was glad to have Agnes there to take the lead. Using that much magic left me exhausted, and the fatigue carried forward into the next day. I spent my morning yawning between claims and desperately chugging coffee. Since finding out I was a witch, I had to eat more than ever. I chided myself for skipping breakfast. Casting spells really took it out of me, and I could barely focus.

At noon, I got in my car and drove up to meet Izzy at the Hastings estate. Lily, Edmund's daughter, was home for the week before school started back up. The drive through the front gate wasn't any less impressive the second time. Everything about the front lawn was impeccable. The trees that lined the driveway were perfectly shaped, their branches arching. During the summer months, it would be truly impressive. I could picture the leaves blocking the sun.

I parked out front and followed Izzy inside. We trailed a short black-haired man who had greeted us at the front door. He wore a white chef's coat that hung open over his lean frame.

"Patty's helping Lily get ready. She said you could hang out here with me until they're finished," he said over his shoulder. His voice had a singsong quality.

We came to a stop in the kitchen. It was almost twice the size of Heather's, which was saying something. She had converted half of her apartment into a kitchen. White granite counters sprawled across the back wall. An island the size of a truck took up the center of the room. Cabinets lined every spare inch of the walls. There were two fridges, one in each of the far corners of the room. Seated with his back to us was another man with shaggy brown hair.

The black-haired man walked behind the island, turned on the faucet, and washed his hands.

"You must be Matteo," I said as I stopped in front of the island. "Is it okay if I put my stuff down here?"

"I am. And you may." Every inch of the man in the chef's coat radiated energy, as if at any moment he was going to explode into movement.

The man with his back to the room turned on his stool. He had a warm but sad smile that was reflected in his blue eyes. He looked like he was around the same age as Matteo, which was in that difficult-to-determine spot between late twenties and early thirties. "Don't mind Matteo. I would be lying if I said he was usually warmer, but today, he's being a bit of a sourpuss."

"I'm Dani." We shook hands.

"Tony."

I settled my bags onto the counter and fished out a folder from one of the pockets. I handed it to Izzy. "A few of the photos I've taken so far. What do you think?"

I held my hands still while she flipped through the photos. Most of the photos I took were for home inspections or the occasional fun outing. I hadn't shared any of my more artistic shots with anyone outside the family since I was in college.

Izzy whistled. My heart skipped a beat. *Was that a good whistle or a bad whistle?*

"These are amazing, Dani. You've really got a good eye."

The tension that had been building in my shoulders released, and I let out a long breath. "Good. Any feedback for future shots?"

She handed me the folder. "I trust your judgment."

I fiddled with the folder, stuffing it into my bag as Izzy stepped away and looked out the windows.

"So, do you both work for the family?" I asked.

Tony laughed. "No, I picked up Matteo from the airport and thought I would pop inside." He gave me a conspiratorial smile. "I'm hoping if I sit here long enough, he'll have something for me to taste test."

"Did you go somewhere fun?" I asked Matteo.

He shrugged. "Visiting family. A week in Kolkata to see my mom's family and a week in Merida to see my dad's. I don't know how they talk me into it every year. It leaves me jet-lagged for days."

"It must be nice to be back home," I said, trying to hide a smile. Tony was right. Matteo was a bit of a sourpuss.

He shrugged again and moved on to chopping spinach. "Merry Christmas. Your boss is dead. You might not have a job soon. That's a great way to come home."

"Knock it off," Tony said.

Matteo dropped his knife and closed his eyes. "What am I supposed to be thinking?"

"That Charlotte loves your food," Tony said.

"One person doesn't need a chef." Matteo slumped against the counter.

I understood that fear. My mom had bounced around between odd jobs for my entire childhood. The only consistent thing had been my gran. Financial insecurity scared me more than chasing killers.

Tony leaned across the counter and squeezed Matteo's

shoulder. "And if she doesn't, you are much too talented to stay unemployed for long."

"Are you sure?" Matteo looked up at him, his dark-brown eyes hopeful.

"Positive." Tony glanced over his shoulder and dropped his voice. "If anyone has to worry, it's my mom."

"Your mom?" I asked.

Tony nodded. "Charlotte's retired. I don't think she's going to need a full-time personal assistant anymore."

"Is that how you started working here?" I asked.

"I don't work here. I'm just visiting."

"And I met this lughead here," Matteo said.

"I practically grew up here," Tony said. "I was finishing up high school when Matteo started. For the first few years, I was just some annoying kid. But I wore him down."

"He did not take no for an answer when it came to an offer of friendship." Matteo snorted.

Tony laughed. "You say that like it's a bad thing."

I rested my hip against the counter and studied them as they talked. Matteo chopped vegetables in quick, precise movements, while Tony lounged at the counter, his shoulders relaxed.

"I know you're just here for the food." The corner of Matteo's mouth quirked up. He was trying not to smile.

My gaze bounced between them. Matteo reminded me of a house cat, and Tony was like a golden retriever. It was an odd friendship but one I suspected Matteo treasured.

"I—"

"Miss Lily is ready for you," Patricia said from behind me. I spun toward her. I hadn't heard her come in.

"Miss Williams?" Her eyes widened. "I didn't realize you were the photographer. If you'll follow me."

I grabbed my bag and trotted after her through the living room and out into the sunroom, with Izzy at my side. Lily lay sprawled across a chaise lounge, her long skirts billowing around her legs and her arms gracefully draped across her lap. Her hair hung in ringlets around her face. It was a dramatic pose, reminiscent of Renaissance paintings. There was a single stool in the center of the room.

Izzy stepped forward and offered her hand. "Miss Hastings, I really appreciate you taking the time to see us. I wanted to first extend my condolences for your loss. I can't imagine how difficult this must be, so if you need to take a break, please don't hesitate to let me know."

Lily glanced between Izzy's outstretched hand and me. She hesitantly reached forward and shook it before resettling in her pose. I set my bags down and pulled out my equipment as Izzy took a seat on the stool.

Izzy pulled out her notebook. "Were you and your father close?"

"He was a busy man, but he always made time for me." Lily held perfectly still as she answered, her eyes focused just over Izzy's shoulder. Only after I snapped a photo did she move. She raised one of her hands and placed it across her chest, her fingers lightly touching her collarbone.

"Is there a particular memory that stands out?" Izzy asked.

"Like a favorite memory?" Lily cocked her head in a practiced pose. She held it until I could get into place to take another photo. "There are too many to pick just one. Daddy was always reliable. He wanted me to live my Broadway dream, and he did whatever it took to help me get there."

I snapped a few photos. She shifted position and held it again. That time, she faced straight forward, and staring out the window, she had a slight misting in her blue eyes.

"He always made me feel like I was a priority. The best tutors. The best dance classes. Voice coaches. Whatever I needed. And he was almost always at my debut performances. Even if he had to duck out occasionally to take a call."

"Did he duck out often?" Izzy asked.

Lily waved the question off as she readjusted in a new pose. "I remember the first time I got a leading role in a school play. I was twelve, I think. He made sure I received flowers at the curtain call. It made everything feel so much more special, you know?"

Izzy jotted a few notes down. "So you shared a love of the arts?"

"We did." Lily nodded. "He took me to Paris for my high school graduation. I don't know how many hours we spent walking the halls of the Louvre or the Petit Palais. I suppose that would be my fondest memory. He was so... thoughtful."

"Is that why he planned to leave you all the art in his will?" Izzy asked.

In less than a second, Lily's face shifted from sad and serene to barely contained fury. She surged to her feet, her hands balled into fists at her sides. "You think I care about a will?" she wailed.

Patricia darted forward and scooped Lily into a hug. She glared at Izzy over her shoulder. "What sort of question is that?"

Lily pushed away from Patricia and flung herself down on the chaise lounge. She crossed her arms over the lip of the chair and buried her head between her hands. The wailing intensified.

"I think it's time that you both left." Patricia stepped between Lily and Izzy.

I shoved my camera into my bag and quickly gathered my things. As I zipped my bag, I glanced up at Lily. She was still wailing, but she peeked out at me from between her fingers. Her eyes were dry. I clenched my teeth. There was something smug about her expression.

After I picked up my bag, I scurried out of the room behind Izzy, with Patricia hot on my heels.

Patricia followed us to the front door and scooted us out onto the porch. She glowered at us as Izzy fixed her coat.

Izzy swallowed and forced an apologetic smile onto her face. She turned toward Patricia and extended her hand. "I'm sorry about that. Interviews can be rough at the best of times, but I know she's going through a lot. If you wouldn't mind extending an apology to her for me, that would be appreciated."

Patricia sniffed. "Questions like that are inappropriate for memorial pieces."

"I'll keep that in mind for the next one." Izzy kept that same friendly smile on her face. "Do you know when Mrs. Edmunds will be available for it?"

"We'll be in touch." Patricia took a step back into the house. "But if I were you, I wouldn't count on there being another interview."

Patricia slammed the door in our faces.

Izzy crumpled. She hugged her coat to her as she shuffled down the steps. I followed her.

"She wasn't actually crying," I said when we reached our cars.

"Do you think she did it?" Izzy asked.

I glanced at the house. Lily wasn't much older than my daughter. But Ethan hadn't been, either, and he still killed Jim Mitchell. If he taught me anything, it was that age had nothing to do with a person's capacity for murder. "I don't know. By the way she talked, it sounded like she got whatever she wanted, anyway. What would be her motivation?"

"She's hiding something." Izzy opened her car door. "Let's keep her name on the list. And add Patricia's. She's way too involved for just a personal assistant."

I nodded.

Izzy climbed into her car and drove away. I took a seat in my car and stared at the house. *Does Patricia know Lily was faking, or is she in there trying to comfort her right now?* I rolled down my window and closed my eyes. I whispered the words to the spell that would heighten my senses.

Everything hit me all at once. The chill wind against my skin caused my face to feel like it was on fire. I winced. The sudden inhalation of breath almost deafened me. *Focus.* I pushed my other senses to the background and concentrated on the sounds coming from inside the house. Matteo and Tony were chatting in the kitchen. The sound of a knife chopping echoed back to me. It was hard to distinguish between the kitchen and the sunroom. But underneath the sound of metal hitting wood was the soft voice of Lily. "I don't want to see them again."

"It's okay, sweetheart," Patricia said. "I'll talk to Lottie. She'll understand."

I tried to maintain focus, but exhaustion rolled through me, and the sounds overlapped too much, so I couldn't make out any particular word. Sighing, I dropped the spell and collapsed into my seat. I grabbed a power bar from my bag and chewed on it as I drove toward Point Pleasant.

Bash was hiding his academic achievements behind a frat boy image. Lily was hiding something behind her damsel-in-distress routine. And Izzy was right. Patricia was too involved for a personal assistant. It was almost like she was part of the family too. And Charlotte? She remained a complete mystery, one I wasn't sure I would get the opportunity to solve.

# CHAPTER 10

My mind was still whirling from my encounter with Lily as I parked in front of the Bizzy Bean. I hugged my coat to my body as I trudged to the front door. Heather was prepping to reopen for the day. I peered at her through the glass and knocked. She let me in.

"You look like you've been having a great day." Heather closed the door behind me.

"That obvious, huh?" My shoulders slumped as she guided me to a table in the back.

The kittens were all passed out on the cat tower, their round bellies full. Star raised her head, slow blinked, and flopped down next to her fosters.

The scent of fresh-baked cookies filled the air. My stomach rumbled. Heather smiled and darted to the kitchen. She returned with a plate of cookies in one hand and a cup of hot cocoa in the other. She set them down in front of me then took a seat.

"The daughter's interview was a disaster," I said as I broke off a piece of cookie. I brought Heather up to speed on my investigation.

She grimaced. "On the bright side, you can take Matteo off your suspect list."

I pulled out my notepad and crossed off Matteo's and Nick's names. While Nick was hard to read, it didn't make sense for him to kill his dad before Edmund left him the whole company. "That still leaves Bash, Lily, Charlotte, Patricia, and their gardener, Penelope. I'm half tempted to take Bash off the list, since he is the one who told us about the change to the will. But he's a self-proclaimed black sheep of the family, studying environmental law. I got the impression he didn't like the rest of his family much."

"What are you going to do now?" she asked.

"I don't know." I shrugged.

"Is there a spell that might help?"

I shook my head. "Heightening my senses didn't help much. The other ones I've practiced are tracking people, purposefully activating my sight, reading the memory of an object, or using a potion to make people feel more relaxed."

"Those sound useful."

"They all require me to either be in the house, to convince someone who doesn't like me to eat something, or... to potentially look like a stalker. If they catch me following them, I think this family would just close ranks even more."

"Why didn't you activate your sight when you were there?"

"It's complicated. And requires some odd materials. They would have looked at me funny if I was walking around the house staring into a bowl of water or a polished obsidian mirror."

"I guess being a witch doesn't always help." Heather slumped and scrunched up her nose. "I could bake some condolence cookies for you."

"Maybe. I think I'm in a bit of a funk. I'm not sure if I could get anyone to eat them."

"My cookies?" Heather widened her eyes and placed her hand over her heart in mock outrage.

I chuckled and took another bite. Her cookies were magnificent. They were soft and chewy in the center. "It couldn't hurt to try."

"Are there any other family or friends you could talk to? Someone has to know something useful." Heather tapped her fingers on the table. "What would probably be even more helpful is if one of them had a frenemy."

I bit my lip to stifle a laugh. Heather had a frenemy in college who made her life very interesting for a while. If there was anything Heather wanted kept secret, her frenemy would make sure it got out somehow. But when confronted, they were always so sweet that Heather couldn't stay mad for long.

"I suppose it's possible Edmund had a frenemy," I said.

"If he doesn't, I'm sure his daughter does." Heather grabbed her phone and pulled up Lily's social media. "She's an aspiring Broadway actress, right? There's always drama among theater kids."

"She is." I inched forward in my seat. "Most of her profile is private, though. But the casting for productions is usually public."

"And whoever she fights for roles is probably the one." Heather finished my thought.

I grabbed my phone and joined her in the search. We scrolled through announcement after announcement and jotted down the names. Each time one of them appeared again, we put a check mark after it. After twenty minutes, we had a list of eight names, but only one of them had multiple check marks next to it—Jasmine Knight.

I found her easily on social media. Her page was as curated as Lily's, except for the occasional candid family photo. Jasmine came from South Seattle. The photos of her family were of large, smiling groups at picnic tables. In a few photos, her father wore paint-splattered T-shirts over jeans and work boots, and her mom had donned the uniform of a local diner. I paused over a photo of Jasmine dancing. She stared straight at the camera and had a hunger in her eyes. If Jasmine Knight wasn't Lily's frenemy, then I would be surprised.

I flipped my phone around so Heather could see the photo.

"It looks like she's in a community theater play over winter break. Its last show is tomorrow, and there are still a few tickets for sale," Heather said.

"You think she'll talk to me?" I asked as I pulled up the theater on my phone. For Seattle, the prices were surprisingly affordable. I bought myself a ticket.

"Doesn't hurt to try," she said. "And if she doesn't, you could always pull in Chris."

"I already talked to him. I don't have enough of an update. What am I supposed to tell him?" I collapsed into my seat. "'Hey, honey, I think this guy may have been murdered.' 'Why's that, dear?' 'Just a feeling.'"

"Or"—Heather leaned forward and grabbed my hand—"'Hey, honey. I think this guy may have been murdered.' 'Why's that dear?' 'He's left-handed, and he shot himself with his right.'"

"There is that." I rolled my head back and stared at the ceiling. "And he would say, 'But wasn't the door locked? Are left-handed scissors enough evidence?'"

"It couldn't hurt to try."

"Maybe you're right. I'm going to sleep on this and decide tomorrow." I sat up. "After I talk to Jasmine."

I left, having eaten only half of one of the cookies. My stomach rumbled as Heather let me out of the café and locked up behind me. I shoved the hunger aside and moved my car in front of my office to pick up Charlie. He almost always insisted on coming into work with me but would quickly abandon me for his favorite sun spots or for Olivia across the hall. I suspected she was sneaking him extra treats.

I ducked into my office to find him. He wasn't lying on his cat shelf. I scanned the room to make sure he hadn't claimed another spot, and I froze. Sitting on my desk was a notebook. One of my gran's notebooks. I stepped into the room and glanced behind me. No one was in the foyer. I closed the door and darted across the room. *Was I really that tired this morning? I can't believe I left—*

My hand closed around the notebook, and all thoughts left my mind. My pulse quickened as my lungs expanded to their fullest. I rocked forward on my toes as a mix of concern and pride filled me. It was the same pride I'd felt when I touched the last book that had been delivered.

I stared wide-eyed at the notebook. I hadn't left that there. It was new.

My hands shook as I opened it and flipped to the last page —notebook three of seven. Someone was sending me my gran's notebooks. The first two I had received in order, but the last book I had received was four of seven. This was the notebook that had been skipped. A grin broke out on my face as I flipped to the first page. *There might be something I can use in here. Grace is going to be so excited.* Faltering, my hands clenched around the book. *I should wait until we're together.* I shoved the notebook into my purse.

I shook out my arms and exhaled slowly through my mouth to calm my nerves. The last book had held the key to solving Jim's murder. Maybe the new one would hold the key to Edmund's. *Does that mean whoever's delivering them knows about my investigations? Are they watching me?* That thought made me slightly less excited. The idea of someone keeping tabs on me was unnerving. *Does that mean they have the Sight too?* I cut off that line of thinking before it went too much further.

*If someone left it, maybe I can figure out who.* I spun in place, my gaze bouncing from photo to photo on the walls. They were all landscapes. My laptop was closed, the camera facing down. The photo of Grace had been shifted on my desk so that her eyes faced the wall. Someone had delivered that notebook and didn't want me to see who it was. They knew enough to move Grace's photo. And there were no other photos or cameras in sight that would be helpful. I gritted my teeth. *Note to self: Add more portraits to the office.* If they didn't want me to see who they were, they would have to take them all. And to do that, they would have to touch more things—and leave more clues.

*More clues... I have a neighbor.*

I turned on my heel and darted across the foyer. Charlie was sprawled on Olivia's desk, between her keyboard and the monitor.

Olivia poked her head out from the break room. She still wore her hair in Bantu knots. Her A-line teal dress covered her from neck to midcalf. "Back for him so soon?"

"I'm about to head home for the day," I said.

She crossed the room and scratched Charlie under his chin as he stood and stretched. "I think I need to get someone else in here. Most of the day, he's my only company."

"Maybe you should talk to Heather about adopting one of her kittens. Having an official office cat would be fun."

"So long as they get along with the official office mascot," she said.

I scooped Charlie up and fitted him into his harness. "Did anyone go into my office earlier?"

"Not that I noticed." She lowered herself into her chair. "Why? Is everything all right?"

*Shoot. No witnesses.* "Someone left me a package. I just wanted to thank them."

"Wish I could be more help." She sat up straight, her eyes

71

lighting up with excitement. "How do you think Charlie would do with a dog?"

"I don't know." I smiled. "We could always schedule a meet and greet if you were thinking about getting an office dog instead."

She grinned. "Zach had dogs from the time he was a baby until he went off to college. I'm sure he would love it if we got one."

"That's a great idea. Especially now that you guys have little Zachary Jr. It would be like he's following in his daddy's footsteps."

We made plans to hold a meet and greet between Charlie and dogs from a local rescue. Olivia was buzzing with excitement when I left. I made a beeline to my car and secured Charlie in the front seat. He curled into his usual spot and watched me.

Before pulling out, I texted Grace.

> **DANI**
> Meet me at home.

> **GRACE**
> Everything all right?

> **DANI**
> I received a new notebook.

Olivia's excitement had been infectious. I drove all the way home with a giant smile on my face. I had a new journal, new opportunities, and possibly a new office puppy. While the investigation was at a dead end for the moment, things were looking up in other ways.

# CHAPTER 11

Grace was sitting on the porch steps when I got home. She jumped to her feet as I pulled into the driveway, and she hopped from foot to foot as I parked. I had barely gotten out of the car when she wrapped her arm around mine and guided me to the front door. "Have you looked at it yet?" she asked.

"I checked to see what number it was, but that's it. I wanted to wait to open it with you."

"Which one is it?"

"Three of seven."

We sat down at the kitchen table, and I pulled the journal out of my purse. I laid it out in front of us. We exchanged a look. She gripped my hand under the table, and I opened it to the first page.

> Dani,
>
> I am so proud of you for making this much progress. I wish I could have been there to go through the books together. It was difficult to figure out what order to write them in or how to group everything. I finally decided to put them in the order I learned them. I hope you continue to master these lessons. Self-

*ishly, I also hope that now that you are further into your jour-
ney, you might understand why I hid things from you and that
perhaps, maybe, you have begun to forgive me.*

*With love,*

*Gran*


I stared at her signature for what felt like a second—or
maybe an eternity. Time contracted and expanded as I held
my breath, staring at the word. In the last notebook, there
had been no such note. *Will this be the last one? Will there be a
note in book five?* Grace squeezed my hand. I exhaled sharply
and turned the page.

We slowly flipped through the book, skimming the
descriptions of the various spells and the theories behind
them. That might have been the order in which Gran learned
magic, but it was overwhelming. I was glad whoever sent
them had changed the order. The notebook was dense, and
each spell was more complicated than the last. Only the first
few spells seemed simple.

The notebook seemed focused on a type of magic called
conjuration. It involved summoning objects, people, or
animals—or banishing them. There was an entire section on
there being another plane of existence, with a big, bold
warning to never try to access it. The last spell was for
summoning a familiar.

"You should cast that one." Grace pointed at the *summon
familiar* spell.

I glanced at Charlie curled into a ball on his cat hammock
that was strung across the kitchen window. He hugged his
paws to his face, covering his nose and eyes. *What if it's not
him?* My heart clenched. *He's been there for me through thick
and thin. He doesn't deserve to be supplanted by another animal.* I
shook my head. "Maybe some other time."

"Why—"

"You should try it," I suggested.

Grace's brow furrowed as she read through the spell. "It's complicated. I don't think I'm ready for it yet."

"I wonder if the Retirees have familiars?" I asked.

She perked up. "I should ask them during the next witches' school lesson. They can tell us what it's like."

"Yeah." I scratched my chin. "I'm not really sure what Gran meant by 'you can sense what they sense.' Like, can I see through their eyes, or is it more like... I'll know when they're hungry?"

"I wonder if they can talk?" she asked as she reread the spell. She scrunched up her nose and harrumphed. "Apparently not. As cool as understanding each other on an instinctual level sounds, I've always wanted a talking cat. Salem was the best part of *Sabrina*."

I tried not to laugh as I flipped back to the second page and tapped the spell to summon an object. "This one looks simple enough."

We read through it again. It was one of the few that didn't require preparation. There were no material components or circles that needed to be created. It was a simple incantation.

Grace followed me into the living room. I grabbed one of the old remotes and set it on the couch. I held the book open in front of me and said the words. On the second word, I knew I had made a mistake in trying to cast again so soon after our long magical session the night before. I had felt low on energy at the Hastings estate when I heightened my senses. Now I was almost completely tapped out. The motes of light spluttered and sank to the floor. I swayed on my feet. The room swam around me. My stomach rumbled, and I crumpled to the ground.

It wasn't so bad on the floor. The hardwood was cool under my cheek. A few lingering motes of light settled into the wood and vanished. My mouth was dry. I tried to swallow and focus on standing, but my limbs didn't want to move.

Grace's face filled my vision as she crouched in front of me. "Mom! Mom, are you okay?"

I closed my eyes and groaned. "I think I overdid it."

The floors creaked. Her footsteps clattered against the kitchen tile. The fridge door opened and closed. A few seconds later, she was back and pulling me up into a sitting position.

"Agnes told me casting magic takes a lot of energy. Did you eat lunch?"

I shook my head.

"Drink this." She shoved a cold glass into my hands.

Orange juice had never tasted so good. I gulped it down, emptying the glass in a few swallows.

"Your blood sugar is probably low." She shoved a Snickers bar into my hands.

"I'm not diabetic," I mumbled.

"Neither's Agnes." Grace frowned and tapped my chest. "But the energy's got to come from somewhere. And it comes from in here."

I pushed myself up and wobbled to the couch. Grace hovered over me as I ate. "When did you learn all this?"

"I've got a lot of free time on my hands." She took the candy bar wrapper from me and disappeared into the kitchen. She returned with a blueberry muffin. "Eat this."

"I think—"

"Eat it." She shoved it toward me.

I took it sheepishly and slowly tore off a chunk. She crossed her arms and watched me until I had finished the whole thing.

"Promise me you won't skip lunch again. Especially on days after we've used a lot of magic."

"This just—"

"Promise me." She glowered at me.

"Fine." I crossed my heart. "I promise."

She relaxed and walked over to the journal I had dropped

unceremoniously on the floor when I fell. She picked it up and flipped to the first page.

"What are you doing?" I asked.

"I'm not the one who skipped lunch." She cocked an eyebrow at me.

"And breakfast." I ducked.

"Mom." Her tone was judgmental. "I'm the teenager here!"

"But we're both still baby witches." I smiled up at her sheepishly.

She pursed her lips. "You should probably eat another muffin."

"How about a protein bar?" I asked.

She shrugged.

I retrieved a protein bar from my stash in the kitchen and sat munching it as she read through the spell herself. Her eyes flicked between the book and the remote on the couch. She cleared her throat and spoke the words to the spell, carefully enunciating each syllable. A flurry of purple and green sparkling lights flew through the air and spun around the remote. It lifted from its spot on the couch and flew straight into her hand.

A grin broke out across her face, and she twirled with the remote outstretched in her hand overhead. "I'll never lose my cell phone again."

I laughed. I couldn't imagine how much time we had wasted over the years searching for keys or our phones. The couch at our old place in Spokane was notorious for eating the remote. Every other day, it somehow got wedged between the cushions but never in the same place two days in a row. It migrated, and we almost always found it after pulling off the last cushion.

I finished the protein bar and stood. The unsteady feeling was gone. "My turn?" I held my hand out for the journal.

Grace narrowed her eyes at me but handed it over. She padded to the couch and dropped the remote. It bounced and landed between the second and third seats. She crossed the room and stood next to me, hovering, as if prepared to catch me again if I fell. I glanced between her, the notebook, and the remote. I really was feeling stronger after eating the snacks.

I cleared my throat and muttered the words to the spell.

The white motes of light were stronger that time. They flowed out of my mouth and swirled around the remote. I held the image of the remote in my head and willed it back to me. It lifted off the couch cushions and floated slowly across the room. It swayed in the air as if buffeted by winds. I continued the incantation and held my hand out. The remote hovered over my palm. I released the spell. The motes of light dissipated, and the remote fell that last half an inch into my waiting hand.

"No more lost car keys," I said, pulling Grace into a hug. We bounced together, chanting "No more lost car keys." Dancing around the house after successfully casting a spell for the first time had become a tradition of ours.

I collapsed onto the couch, wheezing as I laughed.

Grace flopped down next to me. "What do you want to do for dinner?"

"Didn't I just eat?"

"We both could use more food."

My stomach rumbled. *How can I still be hungry?* "Pizza?"

She grabbed the notebook from my hands and held it overhead so she could read it from her position sprawled out next to me.

"What are you doing?"

"Practicing." She said the words to the spell. A few seconds later, her laptop floated into the living room.

I waited until it was safely in her hands before elbowing her in the ribs. "You just didn't feel like getting up."

"It can be both." She opened her laptop and started putting in our usual order.

"Girls' night in?" I asked.

"I get to pick the movie," she said.

"And I get to invite Heather."

She nodded. I grabbed the book from her hands and reread the words to the spell. Grace was right. It could be both. I summoned my phone from my purse and texted the invitation to Heather.

# CHAPTER 12

The silence in my office was almost deafening. All I could hear was the clacking of my keyboard as I worked. The photos from the biohazard cleanup company had finally come in. I scoured through them, poring over every detail. There was a clear shot of the gouge on the floor from the second bullet. And slightly out of focus right next to it was a strange warp on the floor. I stared at it until I went cross-eyed. The hairs stood up on the back of my neck every time I looked at it. There was something important about that photo, but I couldn't tell what. The photo was too out of focus to be useful.

For the first half of the day, I bounced between staring at the photos, checking my phone, and working claim files. By lunch, I had checked my phone almost a hundred times to make sure I hadn't missed a message from Izzy. For the remainder of the afternoon, I had forced myself to stow it in my purse across the room from my desk while I listened to calming lofi music. The urge to check my phone didn't go away, and it had the annoying side effect of keeping me hyper-focused on the time. The minutes crawled by, and when I had to leave to go to Jasmine's show, it felt like I had been stuck at the office for days.

After taking the ferry across to Mukilteo, I drove down to Seattle. I munched on protein bars to keep my energy up. Traffic was like a reflection of my day so far. It alternated between picking up speed and inching forward one car length at a time as everything ground to a halt. It took almost two hours to arrive in the Greenlake neighborhood. I found a place to park and walked three blocks to the theater, arriving just in time to take my seat before the play began.

I had never been to that theater before. There were two stages. The play I was there to see was on the larger of the two. Despite that, it was still cozy. It fit about two hundred people at capacity, and the farthest seat was no more than thirty feet from the action. It had stadium-style seating, so every seat in the house was good.

The cast was small, with only five actors, but Jasmine stood out. She was easily the youngest on the stage. While the others danced and sang beautifully, Jasmine was exquisite. She had star power. I perched on the edge of my seat, enraptured until the curtain fell at the end. I blinked and relaxed into my seat as the other patrons retrieved their coats and filed out.

I dawdled and trailed the last of the attendees. The street cleared until it was just me standing there, with my coat wrapped around me and my collar up to block the chill wind. I shoved my hands into my pockets and stomped my feet to keep warm. Almost half an hour later, the cast and crew emerged from the building, chatting excitedly about the show.

"Jasmine Knight?" I raised my hand to get her attention.

Jasmine's head jerked toward me. She raised a single eyebrow. "Yes?"

"Hi. Sorry to interrupt. I'm working on a piece for the

*Island County Gazette* and hoped you could spare a few minutes to answer some questions."

She glanced between me and the other actors. "What sort of piece? I haven't performed outside of Seattle."

"It involves a friend of yours. Lily Hastings."

Jasmine laughed then froze, her expression shifting from amused to serious in the span of a second. "Does this have something to do with Edmund?"

"It's a memorial piece."

"I didn't really know him well..." She faltered. The rest of the cast stood a few feet away, waiting for her. "We were planning on getting drinks to celebrate. I should probably get going."

"I'm trying to capture what the family was really like." I took a small step forward. "How about this? I'll buy you a cup of coffee, and I have until you're done drinking it to ask my questions."

"If it's a memorial piece for Edmund..." One of the other actors put his hand on Jasmine's shoulder. He had been the main character. On stage, he had been made up to look like an older man, but under the streetlights, he looked younger. The fake white had been brushed out of his hair. "You should do it, Jaz. We'll be two doors down, so you can always join us after."

Jasmine nodded. "There's a coffee shop around the corner."

"Lead the way." I smiled.

The cast hugged Jasmine and continued up the block to the bar. Jasmine turned and led me to a coffee shop half a street over.

I altered my stride so we walked side by side down the sidewalk. "Thank you so much for doing this."

"I'm not sure how much help I'll be," she said.

"What type of coffee would you like?"

"Chai tea, actually."

"Sounds delicious." I held the door to the café open for her. I rarely found coffee as good as Heather's, so a nice tea would be a pleasant change of pace.

I walked up to the counter and placed an order for two chai teas while Jasmine took a seat at a back table. As I carried the drinks over to her, I mumbled the words to the relaxation spell. It didn't alter someone's mood a lot, but it made it easier to get honest answers out of them. Motes of white light swirled between me and the cup and settled into it. Every time I cast spells in public, I was thankful that only witches could see magic. By Jasmine's placid expression, it was clear she wasn't one. I handed her the glowing tea and took a seat across from her.

She held her cup in front of her and inhaled deeply before taking her first sip. The warm glow from the cup transferred to her and settled into her skin.

"So, what can you tell me about Lily?" I took a page out of Izzy's playbook. "What type of person is she?"

"She's a capable dancer and actress. Her singing could still use some work, but with the right piece, she shines." She took another sip of the tea. "She's fine. It's not like she doesn't work hard. But she is someone who has benefited from nepotism."

"How so?"

"Her grandmother was an actress, as was her great-grandmother. They still have some connections in the area. Plus, her father was a big patron of the arts. He's one of the biggest donors for a few of the theater companies around here. That can get you auditions where you otherwise wouldn't get them." She frowned. "It's a part of the industry. You get used to it."

"Did her dad come to a lot of her shows?"

"Every opening night. But he usually ducked out after a few minutes to take calls." She wrapped her hands around her cup and stared into it. "That always made a lot of people feel a little bad for her, to be honest. Everyone knew."

"Was that indicative of the rest of their relationship?" I asked.

She nodded. "I never got the impression Lily liked her family. She accepted their funds. It was all very transactional. Her dad was a checkbook."

I crossed my ankles to keep them from bouncing. There was a slight pressure at the back of my head. I was on the verge of something important. "Do you remember any recent changes?"

Jasmine looked to the side. "Maybe…"

"I promise not to use your name," I said.

She inched forward in her chair until she sat perched on the edge and lowered her voice. "I overheard her talking to her brother. The middle one, who likes to party. She was complaining about their dad changing his will."

I forced my eyes to widen in fake surprise. "A will change?"

"Her brother seemed thrilled about it. But Lily was angry. She kept saying that she had put in the work and deserved more than those who hadn't." Her tone shifted as she imitated Lily. "'What am I supposed to do with a bunch of crusty old art, anyway? It's just like him to completely miss the point.'" Her tone shifted back to normal. "She was on the verge of one of her fits, but her brother talked her down before she exploded."

"Was Lily angry a lot?"

"The first time I got a role over her, she threw a cup at my head. And it wasn't one of these paper ones. I have a small scar on my back from where a piece of the ceramic hit me." Jasmine snorted and took another sip of her tea. "And the second time, she snuck laxatives into my breakfast. I was too sick to perform opening night, and she took the stage in my place. I don't trust her as far as I can throw her."

"Wow." The pressure in my head peaked as Jasmine spoke. A motive and anger issues. Lily went straight to the top of my list.

Jasmine took the last sip of her tea and set the empty mug down. The glow from the spell dissipated as she stood. "Thanks for the tea."

"And thank you for talking to me." I stood and shook her hand. "I hope you have a good time at the wrap party."

I watched as Jasmine left the café and disappeared down the street. The smile on my face faded. I had found my lead suspect, but I had no way of proving it. *What use is finding a thread if I can't pull on it?* I sighed and collected my things. Maybe Heather was right. Maybe I needed to pull Chris into my investigation. I walked to my car and drove home. I had found a motive, but that still didn't answer the question of how she'd killed someone in a locked room.

# CHAPTER 13

I woke up early the next morning to meet Chris for our weekly coffee date. Bob, the sheriff, had punished him for helping me out on my prior investigations by making him monitor a little-used intersection out by Millers Farm. It was on a random day every week, so he could never fully work it into his schedule. It was so early that most of the coffee shops weren't open yet. Fortunately, Heather had taken pity on us and let me have some of her proprietary honey-roasted blend. It still didn't taste as good as when she made it, but it was a close second. I filled a thermos with the freshly brewed coffee and headed out for my date.

The roadways were deserted all the way out to the farm. The sun wouldn't be up for at least another hour. I pulled up next to Chris's cruiser and got out. The wind ripped through the trees. Icy tendrils of air swept past me. I shivered, darted to his car, and threw myself into the passenger seat before slamming the door shut behind me.

I thrust the thermos into Chris's hands. "I forgot gloves, and it is absolutely frigid out there."

Chris chuckled as he poured us cups of coffee. "How's the new job opportunity going?"

I wrapped my hands around the warm cup and slouched into my seat. I tried not to scowl, but it was too early to keep the truth from my face.

"That bad, huh?"

"I think I've lost the gig."

"You want to tell me about it?" He rested his coffee cup on the dashboard while he grabbed a box of pastries from the center console.

"I don't think they liked the interview questions. But we couldn't not ask them about the changes to the will."

He raised an eyebrow. "What? Is someone being written out or something?"

"I don't know." I sipped my coffee. "He died before the changes could go through."

He handed me a pastry from the box. It was a strawberry-and-cream-cheese Danish. "Then why ask?"

I fidgeted in my seat. "We might have reason to believe Edmund Hastings was murdered."

He dropped his pastry into his box and turned to me. "Your bad feeling? Okay. Tell me the facts of the case."

"I wouldn't go so far as to call it a case. I'm just... poking around."

"And what do you have?"

"Not much." I shrugged. "When I did the home inspection, I noticed Edmund had left-handed scissors on his desk. Not just that, but everything at his desk was set up for a left-handed person. But based on where he was sitting, and the bullet holes, he would have shot himself with his right hand. Doesn't that seem odd?"

"A little." Chris scratched his head. "I can make some polite inquiries with the medical examiner. See if he's willing to let Victor help. He's great at finding inconsistencies."

"Thank you!"

"I can't make any promises, though. Especially if the family doesn't want an in-depth autopsy."

My phone dinged in my pocket. I pushed myself back in my seat and fished it out. One new message from Isabel Carter. I bit my lip and opened it up.

**IZZY**
The next interview is scheduled for noon.

My jaw dropped. "We might be back on the case," I told Chris as I pecked out a response.

**DANI**
I thought we wouldn't be allowed back.
How'd you swing that?

**IZZY**
A bit more brownnosing than I would like to admit.

Your excellent photos helped. The editor really liked them and made some calls on our behalf.

**DANI**
That's wonderful!

**IZZY**
There are caveats. We are basically on probation. We've been approved to interview the staff. And if we don't ruffle any more feathers, then we get a crack at the wife.

Izzy sent me the interview location. It was at the estate, and I stowed my phone away. I buzzed with anticipation. We were back on the case.

Chris frowned. "I guess I should be used to this by now."

"I'm going to be careful." I laid my hand over his arm.

"I know. It's one of the things I love about you. You don't give up when something piques your curiosity."

My heart skipped a beat at the word *love*. It was still early days. We hadn't thrown around words like that before. By the way he was fishing around in his pockets, it was clear he didn't realize he had let that word slip. I bit my lip and watched him.

"It doesn't mean I have to be happy about it, though. Saving you from crazed killers three times is more than enough for me." He pulled out a black cylinder on a clip and handed it to me. "Take this. For in case I'm not there next time, if there is a next time."

I stared at the pepper spray in my hands. I'd never used something like it before. "You're so good to me." I closed my fingers around it and held his gaze.

He smiled and leaned in to brush his lips against mine. "You deserve it."

It was strange to think that not too long ago, Chris had been only a friendly acquaintance. We had been friends in high school but drifted apart over the years. He had been best friends with my ex-husband, Ed, when they were younger, and they had gone on annual hunting trips together ever since. After the divorce, I thought he would have taken Ed's side, but he hadn't. I was glad that I gave him a shot at friendship.

I kissed Chris back. The butterflies in my stomach took flight. One of the things I loved about him was he never tried to make me someone I wasn't. I pulled away, a small smile on my lips, and shifted back to my side of the car. I grabbed my coffee and continued to sip it as we talked about our week until the sun rose on the horizon.

# CHAPTER 14

That morning, I spent some time going over my suspect list and reexamining the photos from my home inspection. Even if we figured out the motive for the murder, I didn't know how we were going to prove the means and opportunity. The room was locked. I stared at my photos of the door. It was a dead bolt lock. It wasn't something Edmund could lock then close the door without the key, and he'd reportedly had the only copy inside the room with him.

I chewed on my lip. Obviously, I had to be missing something. I pulled up the diagram of the rooms. It covered a large section of the first floor but not all of it. The interview that afternoon might be our last opportunity to talk to anyone. It might also be my last opportunity to look around the house. I packed my laser measuring device and a small handheld obsidian mirror into my camera bag. If the interview was going to be my only chance, I wanted to make sure I got as much information about the home as possible. And getting a vision or completing the diagram of the first floor would give me ideas.

Having already driven to the Hastings estate so many times, at that point, I barely needed my GPS. I waited at the gate for almost three minutes before someone finally buzzed me in. Izzy drove in behind me and parked next to my car. We walked up to the house together.

"Let's regroup after this one, okay?" Izzy stared straight ahead as she walked.

I nodded then cleared my throat. "Sounds like a plan."

Patricia greeted us at the door and led us through the house and to the dining room. She pulled out a chair and perched stiffly on the edge. Izzy took a seat opposite her, and I put my bags down on the table and set up my equipment to take a few shots. The lighting in the dining room was abysmal.

"Let's get this over with. I'm not sure why Lottie agreed to this. She's got a good heart, and an agreement is an agreement. What's your first question?" Patricia peered down her nose at Izzy.

I crouched next to the table and directed a diffused light at her from the side.

"What type of man was Mr. Hastings?" Izzy asked, pulling out her notebook.

"A good man. A good husband. A good father. He was someone who could always be counted on for giving back to the community." She glowered at me as I readjusted the lights.

I raised my camera and focused on her face. The light box helped, but capturing a good shot in that room was going to be rough. I switched to my digital camera. The deep shadows around her would require more editing than I wanted to do with film. I snapped a few test shots.

"What's your fondest memory of Edmund?"

Patricia shifted in her seat and frowned at me. "Are you done?"

"Oh, I—"

"I heard the shutter go a few times. I think you've got your shot. Go and wait in the sunroom."

Her tone didn't invite an argument. I packed up my stuff and stalked out of the room. The test shots would have to do.

I let the frustration wash over me. A good photo would have been nice, but the real purpose of the visit was to poke around. I chose not to look a gift horse in the mouth. I made my way to Edmund's office and ducked inside.

The heating vent had been closed during the biohazard cleanup. The chill air had seeped in around the windowpane, making the room a good ten degrees colder than the rest of the house. I fumbled with my bag and pulled out the obsidian mirror and the first journal my gran had left me. I hadn't practiced the purposeful activation of my sight many times and didn't remember the words to the spell yet. The first time I cast it, I thought the spell had failed because all I saw was my daughter. In hindsight, the spell had worked as intended. I just didn't know she was also a witch at the time.

Holding the journal in one hand and the obsidian mirror in the other, I quickly reread the spell. I cleared my throat and began. Motes of white light swirled out of my mouth as I spoke. Half of the motes settled over the mirror, and the other half flowed back and forth between my face and the reflective surface. The remaining lights eventually settled over my eyes. *Show me the night Edmund died.* I poured my will into the obsidian glass. *Show me what happened.*

I lifted the mirror and stared into the reflective surface. Images swam across it too fast for me to follow. I gritted my teeth, raised the mirror, and peered into it with one eye as I looked around the office with the other. I spun in place until I was lined up between the spot where the chair had sat and the door.

There was pressure on my back and down my hamstrings as if I were seated. The mirror didn't show the door. Instead, it faced the window, overlooking the rosebushes. The moon was waxing gibbous, almost three-fourths full. A floorboard creaked behind me. When a cool metal pressed against my temple, I turned toward it. My heartbeat quickened.

*Show me who killed him. Show me.* I poured more of my will into the mirror, but the image didn't shift. The reflection and sensations that followed were all from Edmund's perspective. I held my breath and pushed forward, praying that he saw something helpful. Pain shot through me. I dropped the mirror and fell to the floor as tremors ran through my body.

I gasped, my fingers clenching and unclenching. *Why? I always took care of you.* I blinked. *That wasn't my thought.* I scrambled forward and grabbed the mirror. I held it up, desperate to try to replay those last few seconds. But the mirror was clear. The vision had ended.

After grabbing the notebook, I reread the spell. The motes of light swirled and fizzled. The spell would let me see it only once, and I had missed something. He knew who it was. *What did he mean by* I always took care of you? *Lily? He always took care of her, didn't he? Isn't that what she said the first time I saw her?*

I stood and stowed away the mirror and notebook. I pulled out my laser measuring device and stepped into the hall. With the device in hand, I walked through the rest of the first floor, mapping it out as best as I could. It was hard to focus. My mind was distracted by the vision. I didn't think I would ever get used to the sensation of dying. Fortunately, I didn't have much more to map out. I had missed only the bathroom, kitchen, and sunroom on the first visit. My journey ended in the sunroom, which appeared to be a recent addition. I took measurements of all three rooms and pocketed the measuring device.

Once I flopped down in a chair, I stared out the windows at the backyard. *I always took care of you.* That was the first vision where I had heard the victim's thoughts. Did it have something to do with the fact that I was accessing it through a spell instead of letting my divination powers guide themselves?

I picked at my cuticles, turning the vision over in my mind, as I stared out the sliding glass doors into the backyard. It was a bright, sunny day but still frigid. That time of year, the sun was always lying. It looked warm, but I knew the second I stepped outside, my teeth would chatter and my breath would fog.

Movement caught my eye. I slid forward in my seat and squinted out the window. About one hundred feet away from the sunroom was a greenhouse—and someone was inside it.

I glanced at my watch. Izzy usually took about thirty minutes to finish her interviews. I still had time left. And sitting and worrying about the visions wouldn't get me any more answers that day. I left my bag by the chair and let myself out into the backyard.

I wasn't wrong. The sun was lying. I wrapped my coat around me and trudged toward the greenhouse. I stopped outside of it. A woman knelt next to a planter box, her ash-blond hair pulled into a low ponytail. She was almost fully covered. She wore overalls over a long-sleeved shirt, with garden gloves and sturdy boots.

I rapped on the glass.

She looked up and smiled. She stood, pulled off her gloves, and opened the door, letting me inside. It was instantly warmer.

"You must be Penelope."

"Most people call me Nelly." She shoved her gloves into her belt. "And you are?"

"Dani Williams. I'm the photographer. Patricia sort of kicked me out."

"Sounds like Patty. She gets prickly when things aren't going her way, and she's real torn up about Ed." She rested her hip against the edge of a tall planter box. "Is there something I can help you with?"

"I don't know. I just... I was trying to get a better idea of who Mr. Hastings was. Have you worked for them long?"

"Yeah. A long time. Almost fifteen years. I actually live on the property. There's a cottage out back."

"Oh. So you were here the night it happened?" I asked.

She nodded. "I was in bed. Something woke me up. A noise. I couldn't figure out what it was at the time. But then I heard Charlotte screaming and an awful banging sound. By the time I got into the house, she was past hysterics. She was kneeling in front of the door, banging her fists and crying for Edmund to just please open the door."

I covered my mouth.

"The poor woman could barely function. I'm the one who called 911."

"I'm so sorry. That must have been hard. Are you close to the family?"

"You would think so after fifteen years, but... not really." She used her hands when she talked. Her fingers danced through the air as she spread them out wide to emphasize different words. "I mostly keep to myself. I'm not much of a people person. Not usually. Honestly, I think the only reason I got this job is because my dad had it before me."

I slumped. Another dead end.

"Not what you were hoping to hear, huh?"

"The whole family has been pretty tight-lipped. I was hoping someone might tell me more about who he was and not just who they wanted him to be."

She nodded. "You know who you need to talk to?"

"Who?"

"My dad." At her words *my dad*, the pressure in the back of my head went up.

A grin spread across my face. Finally, a thread to pull on. "You think he would mind talking to me?"

"Maybe. He worked here when Ed was growing up and was a lot more sociable. Let me call him. See if he's all right with me sharing his number." She stepped away and pulled out her phone. I turned to the side to give her privacy. After a few minutes, she turned around, a smile on her face. "His name's Cal. Let me know when you're ready for his number, and I'll give it to you."

I entered his number into my phone, my fingers shaking with excitement. "Thank you so much. I really appreciate this."

"Don't mention it." She returned to her planter box, and I retreated to the sunroom to wait.

Izzy finished her interview a few minutes after I got back. I followed her to the cars. We drove off the estate separately but parked half a block away, and Izzy got into the passenger seat of my car.

"How'd it go?" I was buzzing with energy. I could barely contain my excitement.

"Like pulling teeth." Izzy glowered. "She had nothing but nice things to say. It was all so blank and milk-toast that it felt like a prepared statement. I think someone was coaching her."

"It wasn't a complete waste." I filled her in on my conversation with Nelly.

"Have you reached out to her dad yet?"

"I just got the number." I pulled out my phone.

"Well, what are you waiting for? Set up a meeting."

Cal Cooper was as friendly as his daughter and insisted we both come over to brunch. Izzy returned to her car, and I drove to Point Pleasant. While Patricia had stonewalled us, I had found another opening. I couldn't keep the smile from my face the entire way home.

# CHAPTER 15

All week, the calendar app on my phone had been ticking away, counting down the minutes to the next full moon. I stared at it as the number reached zero. I put my phone away and squinted upward. Despite the overcast sky, I could make out a slightly brighter spot in the clouds, which I assumed was the moon. I tried to hang onto the excitement of discovering a new lead earlier in the day. It was hard. I had been half dreading that moment since our last foray into Meredith's house, and the trepidation hadn't gone away. As I sat outside the home, the apprehension gradually drained my joy, leaving only nervous energy.

"So how do you know it's time? Do you feel different?" Grace asked Sarah.

We were all huddled in Betty's truck. Grace, Sarah, and I were in the back seat, and Agnes and Betty sat up front.

Sarah held her hand out. Her mouth moved, but I didn't hear any words coming out. What looked like embers swirled out of her mouth to dance over her fingertips. A second later, a small ball of fire flickered into life over her open palm.

"Wow," Grace and I said in unison.

"I feel it. I don't know how to describe it. It's like most of the month, I'm color-blind, and then suddenly, I can see all the colors again." She closed her fist around the fire, and it winked out.

"Are you girls ready?" Betty asked.

I swallowed. Grace fished her protection amulet out of her pocket and looped it over her head. I followed suit. The black tourmaline stone was warm to the touch. I gripped it as Agnes pulled a vial of oil from her purse.

"The amulets do a good job all on their own, but there are things we can do to boost their effectiveness." She uncapped the vial then used her finger as a stopper as she shook it. She held up her hand. There was a slight smear of oil on her index finger. "It's called anointing. It's a special oil that I can put on the stones, and it'll boost their power until the next full moon."

"How'd you make it?" Grace leaned forward and gripped the back of Agnes's seat.

"I didn't make it," Agnes admitted. "I've had it for a few years. I got it from a member of our coven who passed away."

I held my amulet out to her, and she rubbed the oil across its surface. We took turns holding our amulets out as she slowly shook small traces of the special oil out of her bottle. It was almost half empty by the time she was done. She carefully capped the oil and put it back in her bag.

"Now, repeat after me." Agnes quickly taught us an activation spell.

We all repeated her words three times before we tried the spell. The car filled with light. The motes from my spell settled over my stone. It was as if the stone absorbed the oil. It seeped into the hard surface and vanished.

"And now, drink these." Agnes handed out the protection tinctures.

"Is this all really necessary?" I sniffed at the tincture.

"I don't know if the house was just booby trapped or if it's cursed itself. We didn't get a good enough look when we were here last," Agnes said. "We really don't know what we are dealing with, and I want to keep all of us as safe as possible."

"While putting us in the best position to find clues," Betty chimed in.

I sniffed at the tincture again then swallowed it. It tasted awful. Normally, I didn't mind the taste of rosemary, but something about the combination of rosemary with the mugwort and other herbs left an extremely bitter taste in my mouth.

"All right." I grimaced and opened the truck door. "I think I'm ready now."

We clambered out onto the sidewalk and stared at Meredith Walker's home. The house shimmered and shifted in front of me as the boards over the windows disappeared. The paint still had a faded appearance, but the house looked like almost every other house on the block. It was eerie how normal it looked. *What just happened?* I glanced between the house and the Retirees to see if they had seen the same thing. They gaped at it.

"I'm usually faster at picking up on illusion spells," Agnes murmured. "It makes sense, though. Someone must have made it look like an abandoned property so no one wonders why it sits empty. I'm almost embarrassed it didn't occur to me to check for illusions when we were out here last."

"Who do you think cast the illusion spell?" I asked.

"Maybe my mom? It seems like something she would have done," Agnes said.

"Spells can outlast the person who cast them?" I tried not to gape as I asked the question. Every day I was learning something new.

Betty nodded. "If you do them right. It takes a lot more prep work, and a whole lot more energy."

I took a faltering step forward. Grace slipped in next to

me and grabbed my hand. She squeezed it, and we walked across the street hand in hand. The steps leading up to the front door creaked under me. Grace handed me the key to the house, and I unlocked the front door.

Inside, everything was different. The graffiti was gone from the walls. There were no bottles or sleeping bags littering the floor. Instead, it was like stepping into a time capsule. There was a couch and a coffee table in the center of the room. An old radio sat on a stand in the corner. Every piece of furniture and decoration could have come straight from the 1940s. The feeling of wrongness still hung in the air, but it was muted. The strange comfort I had gotten over the illusory graffiti was gone. We were probably the only people who had been in the house since the curse began.

"All right. Agnes and I will go left. Sarah, you can go right. Dani and Grace, you can take the center." Betty took command again. "Try to keep each other in sight if you can. Let's get in and get out as quickly as we can. Keep an eye out for anything that doesn't look right. And if the space checks out, we'll link up to activate your Sight. If we are all working together, you should be able to look that far back. Dani, you have your obsidian mirror with you, right?"

I nodded.

"Good. I don't want to be here any longer than we have to." Betty grabbed Agnes's hand, and they turned left.

Sarah turned right and disappeared into the dining room.

I squared my shoulders and stepped forward. Grace trailed me as I inched down the hallway that led deeper into the house and ended with stairs that went up to the second floor. My heartbeat quickened, and my mouth went dry when I reached the base of the stairs. I licked my lips and put my foot onto the bottom stair.

A translucent woman appeared at the top of the stairs. She was even ghostlier than before. I could barely make out her outline. Even her wail was muffled as if she was screaming underwater. Grace gripped my arm as the woman flowed down the stairs toward us. I held my breath as she reached me.

The woman passed right through us then flowed out into the living room. I turned and followed her with my eyes. She continued wailing then vanished.

I blinked and looked at Grace. She shrugged. Without a word, we turned back to the stairs. When I put my foot on the first step, the woman appeared again. I ignored her that time and continued to climb. She flowed through us halfway up the stairs. I felt nothing as the eerie light filled my vision and disappeared as it poured out the other side of me.

We reached the top of the stairs. It was a small landing area, with a hallway to our left. Five doors led off the hall-way, three on one side and two on the other.

"Which one?" Grace whispered.

"I don't know. Left to right?" I whispered back.

We crept forward. My hand hovered over the first door-knob as a scream filled the air. My head whipped toward the stairs.

The scream wasn't muffled. It was a real scream, and it was terrified.

I sprinted for the stairs and ran down them, taking the steps two at a time. I stumbled out of the hallway, my head swiveling back and forth. Agnes and Betty stood shocked in the living room. The scream came a second time from the kitchen. I swung toward it and scrambled past the dining room furniture and into the kitchen.

Sarah stood backed into a corner, her hand pointed at the closed basement door.

I looked from her to the door. There wasn't an obvious danger, but the fear in her eyes was real. I inched toward it to get a better look. Sarah darted forward and grabbed my arm and pulled me to her corner.

"Don't touch it," she rasped into my ear.

"The door?" I asked.

She nodded as Agnes and Betty entered the room. Grace hovered behind them, peering into the room.

"What's wrong with the door?" I asked.

"Look at it. I mean, really look at it. All magic leaves a residue." Sarah held onto my arm, so I couldn't move any closer.

Agnes gasped. Betty pulled her into a hug.

I stared at the door. It looked ordinary. "I don't see anything."

"Relax your eyes, like you're looking at one of those optical illusion posters," Agnes suggested. "But as you do it, pour a little bit of your will into it."

I unfocused my eyes and stared at the door. *I need to see. Show me what's on the door. I need to see.* I repeated those words to myself until the door came into focus.

In bright red, emblazoned across the door, was a sigil. It was a circle with three lines in the middle and with another, smaller circle over the lines. "What does that symbol mean?"

"It means we need to leave. Now," Betty said.

Agnes and Sarah nodded and moved toward the dining room.

"Why?" Grace demanded.

"Symbols like that aren't left by just any witch." Agnes pointed at the door. "That's something only left by someone working for the Council."

"Whoever left it is called a Warden of the West."

"But why mark just that door?" I shrugged Sarah's hand off my shoulder and stepped farther into the room. As I slowly turned in place, I kept my eyes unfocused. *I need to see. Show me what's hidden.*

Red symbols flared to life. They covered almost every surface of the kitchen. Red marks were worked into the wood of the floors and flowed out into the dining room.

"They're everywhere," I gasped.

The Retirees bunched together. They held hands as they slowly turned. Iridescent lights intermixed with floating pearls and dancing flames swirled around them.

Sarah shook as their hands dropped, her eyes wide. "A team of Wardens."

Betty shot forward and grabbed me by the arm. She dragged me toward the door. Agnes was already ahead of us, scooping Grace up as she went.

"What does that mean?" Grace struggled against Agnes's grip.

"We'll tell you later," Agnes said.

The Retirees weren't stopping. They ushered us out of the house and slammed the door shut behind us.

Betty white-knuckled it all the way to my house. Every time Grace or I opened our mouths to ask a question, one of the Retirees shushed us. By the time we parked in the driveway, Grace had her arms crossed and wore an exaggerated sullen expression only teenagers were capable of. The Retirees power walked up to my front door. Grace stalked them, and I trailed. I didn't appreciate being shushed, either.

I unlocked the front door. Grace took a seat on the couch, her eyes flicking among the Retirees. Betty stood in the center of the room, fidgeting with her purse, while Agnes and Sarah scrambled around it, casting spell after spell. I stared at them, wide-eyed, with my mouth hanging open. After the number of spells they'd casually cast, I would have been exhausted. Maybe magical stamina increased with practice. That would have been nice.

"What—" I began.

Betty flinched and put her finger to her mouth. "Not yet."

Agnes and Sarah did another rotation around the room. Motes of iridescent light and embers floated around the space, settling into every surface. They collapsed onto the couch next to Grace.

"Can I ask a question now?" I asked.

Betty nodded.

"What was"—I gestured around the room—"all that about?"

"Spells to prevent eavesdropping," Sarah said.

"And other spells to create an illusion of a boring conversation around tea if anyone tries to magically snoop," Agnes added.

"Is that necessary?" I retrieved two chairs from the dining room and offered one to Betty.

She perched on the edge of her chair. "Definitely."

"We don't know if we triggered anything when we went into that house," Sarah said.

"And if we did, we need to talk about what we're going to do before the Council reacts." Agnes slumped into the couch, her head lolling onto the headrest.

"You've mentioned the Council before, but I still don't really know who they are. What are they? And why do they have you all so freaked out?" I asked.

"They're like… the government for witches," Betty said.

Sarah snorted. "You can't just say that without providing any history."

"All right." Betty crossed her arms. "You're the history buff. Why don't you explain it, then?"

Sarah straightened and folded her hands on her lap. "Witches haven't always had a Council or laws governing our behavior. We tended to gather in covens and decided for ourselves what was right and wrong. And for the most part, it was okay. Until it wasn't. A few witches, who had made some not-great decisions, got the attention of the church. When people think of the Inquisition, they usually think of the Spanish one, but in truth, it had been going on for a long time before that."

Sarah had been a teacher when she was younger, and it still showed. It felt like I was back in elementary school. I tried not to fidget through her explanation.

"Do they really need this much history?" Betty asked.

Sarah narrowed her eyes and continued. "We came up with the laws first. A bunch of covens got together and voted on them. They were the three things everyone could agree were wrong or just bad ideas." Sarah ticked them off on her fingers. "Never permanently alter another's mind, body, or spirit without consent. Never violate the natural order of things. And never make deals with Outsiders to augment your power."

I still didn't entirely know what Outsider meant, but with the most recent book from my gran, I was beginning to get an idea. There were parallel realms of reality out there, and things lived on those planes. I suspected it was those things I wasn't supposed to make deals with, which seemed like a good idea. It hurt my brain to think about it too much, but I imagined it would be like mixing oil and water. They were just too different.

Sarah dropped her hand into her lap. "We thought, maybe naively so, that witches would self-police. But they didn't. And then the Spanish Inquisition happened. And the witch trials. The only way for witches to stay safe was to stay off the radar of the church and of regular people. A bunch of powerful muckety-mucks basically decided if the entire witching community wasn't going to regulate themselves, then they would do it for us. And the institution they created to do that, the Council, gained momentum. It took on a life of its own, and now it's something we all have to deal with."

"Because the alternative is worse. Let's be honest," Agnes chimed in.

"The alternative is worse," Sarah agreed. "The Council helped end the witch trials. And in this modern age? I don't know if people are truly that much more accepting. And if they aren't, it would be catastrophic for people like us."

"So, if they are here to protect us, doesn't that make them the good guys?" Grace asked.

"Yes? No? It's not that black and white." Sarah twisted in her seat and faced Grace. "The way they keep that peace is they are unforgiving when it comes to any law being violated. There was a town in Idaho in the sixties. There was one witch who violated the laws. One. But when the Council arrived to deal with it, they didn't just punish her. They punished every witch in the town. Because they had the power to stop her and didn't."

A silence fell over the room. *Every witch in town? How many were there?* I opened my mouth and closed it. I wasn't sure what to ask first.

Sarah cleared her throat. "It's not fully known what the punishment was, but there are guesses. One day, there was a town with sixteen witches. And the next, they were all gone. It was almost like they never existed. No one has ever seen or heard from them since."

"And don't forget what happened in Wisconsin," Agnes said.

"What happened in Wisconsin?" I asked.

"Out there, it was a Warden of the East. They're not as harsh as Wardens of the West." Betty wrapped her arms around herself. "After a young witch messed up, they came in, permanently stripped her of her powers, and turned a reporter who had caught wind of her follies into a dog."

"Isn't that against the rules?" I asked.

"Well, that's the thing about Wardens," Sarah said. "They're the only ones allowed to break them."

"That doesn't seem fair." Grace threw her arms into the air.

"It isn't," Betty said.

"It's what keeps all of us safe." Sarah picked up where Betty had left off.

"And for centuries, it's worked," Agnes finished.

"Well, isn't this curse thing against the rules?" I inched

forward in my seat and looked from Retiree to Retiree. "Doesn't that mean they could help?"

"No. That would go against the fourth, unspoken, law," Betty said.

"What's the unspoken law?" I asked.

"Never, and I mean never"—Betty looked between Grace and me—"get the attention of the Council."

"You don't just ask the Council for help." Sarah stood and paced the room. "And it's not like they don't know. Whatever happened here, whatever caused this curse, was so bad that it got a team of Wardens to work together. And that's almost unheard of. If they were going to help, don't you think they would have by now?"

Grace picked at the edge of the couch cushions. "So they haven't done anything, and you haven't done anything about the curse either? Is that right?"

"We don't know how to fix it, so what were we supposed to do?" Agnes asked. "Flail around and hope we find the right answer?"

"So I'm right, then, huh? No one has ever tried to do anything about this curse?" Grace gripped the cushion.

The Retirees exchanged glances. Their eyes darted back and forth among one another until both Sarah and Agnes were staring straight at Betty.

Betty glowered and slumped into her chair. "I wouldn't go so far as to say no one."

Grace sat bolt upright. "Someone's tried to do something about it before? Why didn't you tell us that?"

"It didn't work." Betty lowered her gaze to the floor. She studied a spot next to her feet.

"What happened?" I asked.

"Mel didn't tell us the details," Betty said, shifting uncomfortably under my gaze. It still felt odd to have my gran referred to by her first name. To me, she had always been Gran. "But whatever it was, it broke Lori. She was a vibrant woman one day, and the next... Well, she was just never the same."

"Lori?" Grace's head swiveled toward me. "You mean my grandmother?"

I gritted my teeth and stared pointedly at the floor.

"Yes." Betty joined Sarah in the center of the room. They clung to each other, their breaths held as they stared at me.

"I've never met her. Is she—"

"I don't want to talk about her." I cut Grace off.

Grace furrowed her brow.

The entire room stared at me. I fidgeted in my seat but kept my eyes on the floor. I didn't want to meet any of their eyes. Grace didn't know what Lori was like, but they all did. And they all pitied me for it.

Grace stood and stepped in front of me. "You never talk about her."

"Just drop it," I pleaded.

"If this experience has taught me anything, it's that keeping secrets is never a good idea. Is she still alive?" Grace crouched in front of me.

I hugged my arms to my body and jerked my head away from her.

"If she's so bad, then why is there a photo of her hanging in the living room?" Grace put her hand on my knee.

"Some things are just too painful to talk about." I stood and turned toward the fireplace. My mother's face stared down at me from the mantel. It was our last good day together. Me, my mother, and Gran were all at the mall while I was very pregnant with Grace. Clearing my throat, I blinked back tears. "I think I'm tired. I'm going to go to bed."

"Mom, I—"

I lowered my head and darted out of the room. Charlie stood waiting for me at the head of the stairs. I picked him up and pulled him into a hug.

"Lori lost it when your mom got her powers. And after

108

that, she… It's not really our place to say, but… she wasn't a good mother after that." Betty's voice, although muffled, carried up the stairs.

"Give her time. I'm sure she'll come around once she's had time to process," Sarah added.

I retreated to my bedroom and closed the door behind me. With Charlie still clutched to my chest, I crawled into bed. Lori had stopped being my mother when I was thirteen. I thought briefly that she had changed when I was pregnant with Grace, but I was wrong. The thought that I was treading the same path that had changed her was almost too much to bear. *If we keep going, am I going to abandon Grace too? I needed you, Mom. I needed you. Why wasn't I enough?* I buried my head into Charlie's side, my tears wetting his fur.

# CHAPTER 16

I crawled out of bed an hour early. I was still emotionally raw from the night before and wasn't prepared to talk to Grace, so I quickly showered and got ready. Charlie lay on the bed, his front paws crossed in front of his face, and peered at me as I tiptoed around the room to get dressed. He followed me out into the hall. He scampered ahead of me to Grace's door, where he stopped and looked pointedly from me to the door and back again. I crept past him toward the stairs. He trailed me to the top of them. I could feel his eyes burrowing into me as I padded down the steps with my shoes in hand. At the bottom, I glanced up at him. He sat there, his eyes intent on me, his ears forward. He turned and stalked away, his tail swishing. I hung my head. Even my cat was disappointed in me. I couldn't make myself have that conversation. Not yet. Maybe keeping my mother's photo up had sent the wrong message. But I couldn't bring myself to pull it down, either.

I slipped out the front door and put my shoes on once I was on the porch. I wrapped my coat around me and dashed to the car. My meeting with Cal and Izzy wasn't until ten o'clock, so I had plenty of time to kill. I drove to the office and caught up on a few claim assignments while I waited, and at nine o'clock, I drove up to a small fifty-five-plus community on the outskirts of Coupeville.

The community consisted of a few clusters of tiny homes, with well-manicured lawns, around much larger community buildings. I parked across the street from Cal's home and waited for Izzy to arrive. He lived in a tiny home, like the rest of the community, but his lawn was more colorful than those of the rest. Hardy winter plants dotted the yard. He had enclosed his front porch, turning it into a makeshift greenhouse, which was filled to the brim with flowering plants.

Izzy pulled up behind me, and we walked across the street to knock on his front door.

"Oh, shoo. Shoo. Back up, back up," a deep baritone voice said from inside. I recognized it from my conversation with Cal the day before. He opened the door. Three small miniature pinschers darted around his legs. He clicked his fingers, and they came to a sudden stop and sat down. "Sorry about the little ones. We don't get a lot of new people, and they can get a little excited. You must be Dani."

I held my hand out. "They're adorable. I'm Dani, and this is the reporter I told you about, Isabel Carter."

He had a firm handshake. He smiled, and his face dissolved into smile lines. The joy filled every inch of his face. "I don't think I've ever spoken to a reporter before."

Izzy smiled and shook his hand as well. "We're just regular people."

He laughed and stepped outside. He pulled the door closed behind him. "I'm sure that's true. Except you get paid to repeat what people tell you."

"Only if it's true. Or at least the good ones do that," Izzy said.

He locked up, and we trailed him, heading toward the community center in the heart of the cluster of buildings he lived in. "I can't promise the food will be good," he said over his shoulder. "But I can promise that it will be plentiful. And cheap."

It was around brunch time, and the community center bustled with people. The central room was a large meeting space with tables scattered throughout. A long counter that overlooked an industrial kitchen on the other side took up the back wall. We followed Cal to the counter and put in our orders, then he led us to a table near the windows so he could see outside while we talked.

"I understand you had some questions about poor Edmund." Cal unfolded his napkin.

"Yeah." I forced myself to relax into my chair. My years of interviewing people for claims had taught me that people responded to the energy you put out, and if I couldn't make myself relax, at least looking like I was relaxed had a similar effect. "We've talked to a few family members and current staff, but it's been hard to get a feel for who he really was. We were hoping you could help with that."

"I haven't worked for him in years. Most of what I know is probably out of date."

The waiters arrived with our food. Cal hadn't been lying when he said it would be a lot of food. They had piled my plate high with hash browns, scrambled eggs, and an assortment of breakfast meat. Luckily, the flavor wasn't as bad as Cal had led on. But it was hard to mess up breakfast food. I dug in.

"With memorial pieces, it's good to capture a full picture. That includes who they used to be. Has Edmund changed a lot?" Izzy pushed a piece of fruit around her plate.

"Oh yes. Edmund used to be like Bash. He was a free spirit. He partied and liked to push against his father's expectations. But over time, he turned into his dad." Cal chewed on his food thoughtfully. "His dad was harsh. He had demanding standards. I think he broke Edmund down until he was the son he wanted. It's sad, really. Watching Nick, I feel like he's going down the same road. There is so much pressure in that family to keep up appearances that you eventually lose parts of yourself."

"What do you mean by that?" I asked.

"Nick's engaged to Miss Lauren Davis. As a former employee, I get invited to the big events like engagement parties and the like." He reclined in his seat and stared out the window. "But when you've been around people their whole lives, you get a feel for things. And it didn't feel like they were in love. It was a business decision. Miss Davis is the heir to Alton's Lumber and Hardware. A merger like that would make them the biggest lumber company in the Pacific Northwest."

"When did Edmund change?" I asked.

"When he got back from college at the end of his senior year, he had Charlotte in tow. The parties stopped. He dropped almost all of his hobbies. Took up golf. It was almost overnight. One day he was fun-loving Eddie, and the next he was a carbon copy of his dad."

Izzy picked up a slice of orange from her plate. "Was Charlotte his Lauren?"

"In a manner of speaking. Charlotte always had a brilliant mind for business. Much better than Edmund. She filled in all the areas he lacked." Cal sat up and pointed his fork at us. "That doesn't mean Edmund didn't love Charlotte, mind you. While at its core it was a practical decision over one made by his heart, he still cherished her. Was still faithful to her and worked his tail off to be a good family man. So don't you go feeling sorry for her. If anyone in that whole situation deserves pity, that would be Patty."

My heart quickened, and my hand clenched around my fork. I willed my body to stay still to hide my excitement over that last sentence. "Were Patty and Edmund an item?"

Cal nodded. "Before he went off to college. He never told his dad about it. I doubt anyone else really knew. Their love affair was a secret. When he got back for summer break his sophomore year, she made a big show of having moved on. He was really broken up about it. I think he had been looking forward to me sneaking her into the house so they could meet up again. But when he left for school in the fall, I could tell she still cared about him. Listless for days. But she was practical too. She knew she couldn't wait around for him forever, especially if she could never officially be his girl. It just took her becoming friends with Charlotte for her to really get over him."

"How did you sneak her in?" Izzy asked.

"It was easy. Back in the 1920s, people used the house for rum running. They shipped it in on fishing boats from Canada. There are secret tunnels in and out of that place. Anyone who lived in that house long enough learned about them. The kids used to play in them." He chuckled and took a long drink from his coffee. "Edmund joked about sealing them up before the kids became teenagers and started sneaking out of the house like he did. With the way Bash and Lily are, I'm sure he had to for his own peace of mind."

"Where are they?" I leaned forward in my seat and held my breath, waiting for him to answer. My mind was spinning at a mile a minute. The warp in the floor. I hadn't been able to figure out what it was in the biohazard cleanup photo. But it was what an old floor would look like if an ill-fitted door had opened over the floor repeatedly for years. It was the location of the secret tunnel. It had to be.

"I don't know where all of them are. I didn't go in the house much. But I know where one lets out."

I pulled up a map of the area on my phone, and he pointed it out to us. There was a secret tunnel that opened up at the back of the property, about fifty feet from the shore.

Trying to calm my nerves, I sipped my water. Cal was a nice guy who liked to talk, but it was a struggle to sit through the rest of the conversation. I was too excited about his revelation of a secret tunnel. I wanted to get my laptop and put together the diagram of the first floor to check for hidden passages or to go to the spot he pointed out and search for tunnels. But instead, I made small talk and half listened as he told amusing stories from Edmund's youth. Izzy dutifully wrote them all down.

At the end of brunch, we walked him back to his tiny home and returned to my car. Izzy sat in the passenger seat.

"If there's a secret tunnel in that house, I bet there are unusual blank spaces in the diagram." I grabbed my computer and opened up my estimating software. I already had the measurements from my initial inspection, and I had managed to get the measurements for most of the other first-floor rooms when we were there last. It was just a matter of updating my map.

Izzy sat with her left leg under her. She angled her body to the side, watching me work.

I plugged in room after room, filling in the spaces. I chewed on my bottom lip as the diagram resized and adjusted with each new addition. After I added the last room, we stared at the screen. There was an empty space, about five feet wide, between the dining room and office.

"Holy moly. He was right," Izzy said.

"We've got to check it out." I stuffed my laptop into my bag. "If we can find the entrance Cal mentioned, it might be the proof we need to show the cops that it wasn't a locked room."

Izzy nodded and opened her car door. "I'll follow you there."

She dashed to her car. While she got situated behind her steering wheel, I texted Heather.

I pocketed my phone and pulled away from the curb.

It was a twenty-minute drive up the coast. I looped around Penn Cove, its short, pebbly beach covered in driftwood. I found a parking spot close to the place Cal had marked on the map and got out of the car. It was a narrow two-lane road, with thick trees along one side and glimpses of water through the brush on the other. Izzy pulled to a stop behind me, and we both got out.

I fished my phone out of my pocket and followed its map to the correct location. I looked between my phone and the side of the road. The vegetation was dense, and the ground cut off sharply as it sloped toward the water.

"Is it down there?" Izzy hovered a few inches away. She peered over my shoulder and shifted from foot to foot.

I glanced at her feet. She was dressed appropriately for an interview but not for hiking. In those black pumps, she could fall easily and break an ankle.

"I think so." I stared down the slope. Gritting my teeth, I took a tentative step off the road.

The ground was firmer than it looked. The exposed rocks were buried deep in the earth, and the thick grass and roots kept everything in place. I grabbed a nearby branch and lowered myself into the ditch, one careful step at a time. I reached the bottom. Izzy was a good twelve feet up, hovering at the edge of the road. I held my thumb up, and she nodded.

I turned back to the ditch and inched forward, my feet sliding over the mossy earth.

The bottom of the ditch was overrun with greenery. Looking for that tunnel entrance was like searching for a needle in a haystack. *What does a tunnel entrance even look like? Has the entrance become overgrown like everything else?* I closed my eyes and breathed in deep. The scent of the ocean filled me. I tuned that out and focused on my body. If I couldn't find it with my eyes, maybe I could find it with the Sight granted to me by my witchy heritage. I took a faltering step forward, then another.

I held my hands out in front of me. The underbrush scraped against my pant legs, the creeping branches clinging to the fabric. Each step was a battle. I yanked my foot up and slowly inched forward until I found good ground and repeated the process with the other leg. There was a tingle at the base of my skull. As I took another step, the pressure at the back of my head increased, and the hair on my arms stood up.

Slowly, I turned. *Only a few more steps.* I held my breath between each step so I could concentrate on that feeling. The pressure grew, and a shiver went down my spine. I stopped and opened my eyes, and I was facing the side of the hill. It was even steeper there, going almost straight up. Vines covered the entire hillside. I reached forward and pushed my hand past the foliage. There was an open space on the other side.

"I think I found it!" I yelled up to Izzy as I shoved the foliage aside.

Before me was a black hole. My heart skipped a beat. *This is it. We found the entrance.* I grabbed my cell phone and switched on the flashlight function. I pointed it into the hole.

Concrete greeted me.

About two feet into the tunnel was a wall built of concrete retaining blocks. I slumped. It was the entrance of the tunnel, but it had been bricked over. I stepped in closer and peered at it. Moss grew between the stones. It had been there for a while. The entrance wouldn't have been an option to get into the house undetected.

I stepped back and trudged up the hill.

"Well?" Izzy clasped her hands in front of her.

"I found it all right." I huffed. "But it's been closed off for years by the look of it. Edmund must have gone through with his promise to seal it."

"Shoot."

We walked to our cars. Izzy climbed in next to me. We stared silently ahead, mulling over the possibilities.

"It doesn't mean the secret passage is out entirely," Izzy said finally. "He might not have sealed them all up. There might be another one."

"Our best bet is to find the entrance in the house." I grabbed the laptop from my bag and opened the diagram again. "If we can get back into his office, we can look for it."

"This might be a good time to mention that I got Charlotte on the schedule." Izzy smiled.

I relaxed into my seat. We could still do this. We could still prove that Edmund wasn't alone in his office. "All right. Let's play it like we did with Patricia. I'll take a few photos and go wait in the sunroom until you're done. So long as no one's hovering, I should be able to slip inside and check if it's there."

"Who do you think did it?" Izzy asked.

"I don't know yet." I frowned. "The family's hard to read. I think it's safe to take Matteo and Nelly off our suspect list. Matteo was out of town, and Nelly didn't read like she had anything to hide. And if she did, why point us in the direction of someone who knew about the tunnels?"

Izzy nodded. "Bash feels unlikely to me too. While he wasn't grieving, he seemed genuinely bummed that his dad died before changing his will. If he was going to do it, he would have waited."

"That leaves Nick, Charlotte, Patricia, and Lily." I ticked their names off on my fingers. "If Cal was right and Nick is going down the same path as Edmund, he might have done it as a last-ditch effort to get out of turning into his dad. But if he did, why is he still moving forward with the wedding? He doesn't feel right to me."

"Maybe he's waiting to call it off," Izzy suggested. "He seems like a planner. Why draw attention too soon?"

"You could be right." I mentally added him back on my list. "We haven't spoken to Charlotte yet, but by all accounts, she's brilliant. She could have staged things or had help. Patricia used to date him. But over twenty years is a long time to be a spurned lover. Why now? Which leaves Lily. She was evasive during the interview."

"She also complained to my editor. She's the reason we almost got kicked off the story."

"And she was upset about the change to the will," I added.

"How do you know that?"

I grimaced and filled her in on my interview with Jasmine Knight.

"Evasive and anger issues?" Izzy whistled.

"So, Lily? Our number one suspect?" I asked.

Izzy shifted in her seat until she was staring directly ahead. She straightened her shoulders and narrowed her eyes. "Agreed. Lily is at the top of our list. Let's see if she's still there after our talk with Charlotte tomorrow."

With that, she got out of my car and strode down the street to her own.

I closed my eyes. *I always took care of you.* Edmund's last thought played through my mind. The sadness and feeling of betrayal clung to the words. He had been so surprised. Lily made sense, but it didn't make my heart ache any less. Betrayal by a loved one was something I understood all too well, and while I didn't know Edmund, that connection made me want to find answers for him even more.

# CHAPTER 17

The Hastings estate didn't get any less impressive. Instead, it somehow managed to be more intimidating with every visit. I swallowed and stared at the house as Izzy and I walked up the front steps. I had a distinct feeling of being unwanted. I raised my hand to press the doorbell. My finger was an inch away when Patricia yanked the door open. She glared at us, her hazel eyes icy with distaste.

"You're late." She scowled and ushered us inside.

"Oh, I'm sorry." Izzy smiled apologetically. "I must have missed a message from you. I had noon on my schedule."

Patricia marched through the house. "Lottie has another meeting soon, so this will have to be quick."

We scrambled to keep up with her as she strode ahead of us up a flight of stairs. I glanced at my watch. It was 11:55 a.m. By the schedule, we were a few minutes early. And I doubted Izzy would have missed a message. She checked her phone every few minutes, like clockwork.

We came to a stop outside of an office. Patricia knocked and ducked inside. I strained to hear the conversation, but it was a thick wooden door. The voices were too muffled for me to hear clearly. *Should I heighten my senses?* I glanced at

Izzy. I didn't want her being weirded out by me mumbling to myself. Last thing I needed was a reporter asking me awkward questions. I sighed and stood, waiting in silence.

After almost a minute, Patricia popped into the hall. "Mrs. Hastings will see you now."

I followed Izzy into the room. Charlotte's office was very different from her late husband's. A single bookcase was half filled with awards and family photos. A single row of accounting books took up the center row. Short wooden filing cabinets filled the rest of the walls, with paintings hanging above them. It had been a while since I had taken any art history classes, but the artwork reminded me of the baroque period. All the figures stood in dramatic poses, with deep shadows obscuring the background.

Charlotte sat behind a large wooden desk, looking as dramatic as the paintings. The curtains were drawn, and a desk lamp illuminated her face. She sat with her hands clasped in front of her on her desk. Her blond hair was pulled into a side bun. She gestured to a single chair across from her, which Izzy took.

I set my equipment down in the back of the room and set up lights as Patricia backed out of the room.

"Thank you so much for—" Izzy began.

Charlotte held up her hand. "I do not have the time or energy for inane conversations. You are here because I allow it. Whatever questions you have planned, at the end of the day, are meaningless. We are both aware of the fact that I have final approval on whatever story is published."

My eyes went wide. I stared at my camera, my hands shaking as I fiddled with the settings. *Is that one of the caveats? Why would Izzy's editor even agree to that?*

"I understand." Izzy smiled again.

It was one I was beginning to recognize as her purely professional smile. The warmth didn't reach her eyes. Not really.

"I am still hopeful that my piece will capture Edmund exactly how you remembered."

Charlotte snorted. "You say that like it's a good thing." She leaned forward in her chair, her green eyes studying Izzy. "You know what? Because I can, and because I will never approve it being printed, I'll tell you what being married to Edmund was really like. It would be nice to get it off my chest. He was cold and distant on the best of days. It was lonely, and he didn't seem to care that my only real friend was my assistant. We hadn't been in love for years. I can't even remember the last time we shared a bed. For the last year, the only time we really saw each other was at business meetings."

There was a fire in her eyes. I tilted my camera up and took a candid shot of her.

"Well, until the last two months, anyway. I thought he had changed. We went on our first date in ten years. He talked about us stepping away from the company together. He said we were going to travel like he always promised we would when we were engaged. I thought I had my old Edmund back. I even stepped down as CFO to make plans for our retirement." She sat back. Her eyes glistened. "I am so angry with him. Why promise me a happy ending after all these years if he didn't mean it?"

I took a second candid shot. It wasn't anger in her eyes. It was grief—a grief I recognized. There was something hard about the final disappointment in a relationship, especially when it followed a hopeful moment.

I stood from my spot. "Mind if I take a few close-up shots?"

Charlotte nodded and dabbed at the corner of her eyes. She cleared her throat and shifted in her seat until the lighting was even more dramatic. Half her face was in shadow. Her green eyes were startling in their intensity. I took a photo straight on without a flash. I wanted to capture that perfect shadow and raw emotion.

I lowered my camera and looked at the shot on the screen. It was perfect. I snapped two more shots just to be sure then packed up my stuff. "Is it all right if I wait in the sunroom? You've got such a beautiful backyard."

Charlotte nodded.

As I retreated from the room, Izzy said, "You have my condolences for your loss. I can't even imagine what you're going through. So thank you for taking the time to talk to me. While I'm not sure what all will go into the article yet, the first question I like to ask is for you to tell me who Edmund was. What type of man was he?"

I closed the door behind me and made my way to the stairs. I peeked down to see if Patricia was waiting on them. She was nowhere in sight. I tiptoed down the steps and padded to Edmund's office. The coast was clear, so I ducked inside and pulled the door closed behind me.

The room was unchanged from my earlier inspection. I pulled my phone out of my pocket, opened up the photos from the biohazard cleanup company, and swiped through them until I found the shot I was looking for—the slight warp in the floor. I padded over to the bookcases and held the photo up as I crept down the line of books, comparing the photo to the shelf. There was a distinctive blue spine in the photo. I stopped when the books in the groove's photo lined up with the books on the bottom shelf.

The office was dimly lit. The curtains had been drawn, leaving the room in heavy shadow. I couldn't turn the light on, so I flipped on my phone's flashlight app for guidance. With my fingers splayed, I felt up and down the edge of the bookcase. I lingered over the spines of the various books. My inside quivered, and my stomach churned as an icy feeling settled over me. Anxiety radiated off those books. I continued my search down. On the second-from-the-bottom shelf, that feeling shifted. Warmth spread through my body. My heart drummed in my chest as my adrenaline surged. The emotional residue left on that book was elated. I pulled the book out, and hidden behind it was a lever.

I held my breath as I pulled on the lever. The door swung toward me. I covered my mouth to muffle the excited sounds that tried to escape my lips. I had found it—a secret passageway in Edmund's office.

The floorboards creaked in the hall. I lunged and pushed the bookcase closed and frantically shoved the book back into place as the door opened behind me. I spun, my heart leaping into my throat.

Izzy stepped into the room. I slumped, exhaling sharply. The sudden dread that had filled me at the sound of the creaking floorboard dissipated, leaving me drained.

"What are you doing here?" I whispered.

Izzy scurried toward me. "Charlotte was called to her meeting early. We probably only have a few minutes to snoop. Have you found anything yet?"

I turned and crouched next to the bookcase, removed the book from the shelf, and pulled on the lever.

Izzy covered her mouth just as I had. There was a difference between knowing there was a secret tunnel in a house and actually seeing it. This was huge.

I pulled the bookcase all the way open and held my phone up to look inside. The space behind the wall was narrow, maybe only four feet wide, revealing the back side of shiplap walls. A thick layer of dust clung to the beams. I pointed my makeshift flashlight at the floor, and the dust had been disturbed. Someone had been inside recently. I stepped inside. The hallway extended a few feet in front of me then became a set of stairs going downward.

Izzy followed me inside and trailed after me as I crept toward the stairs. The air inside the wall was stale.

"Where do you think it goes?" she asked.

"I don't know." I glanced at my watch. "Let's check it out. Let's see how far we can get in a minute. If we don't find anything, we'll head back."

Izzy nodded and clutched my arm as I descended the stairs.

There were no lights in the hallway, no cracks or windows for sunlight to penetrate. Once we were off the stairs, the dim light from the open bookcase above disappeared, leaving us in darkness. The light from my phone was weak and lit up only a few feet in front of me. There could be anything down there, and we wouldn't know until we were almost on top of it.

We shuffled down the passageway. The walls shifted from shiplap to stone. I glanced from side to side as we moved along. Like everywhere in the region, moisture had infiltrated the tunnel. The air was damp. I covered my mouth with the edge of my coat and inched forward.

Up ahead, rock ground against rock. My heart raced in my chest. *What if there's someone down here with us?* I fumbled in my pocket and pulled out the pepper spray Chris had given me. I held it up next to my phone and took another faltering step forward.

A stone from the wall sat in the middle of the passageway. Beyond that, there were more stones. I bent over the stone, holding my phone out as far as it would go to see ahead. The tunnel side had collapsed, and beyond that, just barely visible, was a concrete retaining wall sealing off the end. *What happened here?* I stepped over the rock and squinted into the hole.

Something darted across the tunnel in front of me. I squealed and jumped back, dropping both my phone and the pepper spray.

"What was that?" Izzy scrambled backward down the hall, taking her flashlight with her.

I stood there in the dark, my eyes wide and palms sweaty.

"I don't know. It… looked like a groundhog. Or an enormous rat."

In the darkness, there was a slight glow around the spot where my phone had fallen. I inched toward it. I paused, my ears straining for any movement. Silence greeted me. I lunged, grabbed my phone from the floor, and scurried back. I held my phone out in front of me. The flashlight illuminated the piles of rock and earth. Nothing moved. I swung my phone from side to side. Whatever had darted across the tunnel was gone. Or hiding.

"We should head back," I whispered.

Izzy nodded, and we returned the way we came. I trailed her. Every few feet, I turned and checked the passageway. The hair on the back of my neck stood up, and the pressure at the back of my head pulsated. *What are you trying to warn me about?* I slowed my pace and tried to concentrate on the sensations in my body. My intuition was screaming danger, but I couldn't tell if I was moving toward or away from it. I shook my head and pushed forward. Sometimes, the only way out was through.

I climbed the stairs up into Edmund's office and nudged the bookcase open again. I winced as the light from the room stung my eyes. The sudden brightness made it difficult to see. I blinked rapidly, trying to clear my vision.

"Why'd you turn—" The sentence was half out of my mouth when my gaze landed on Izzy. She lay sprawled across the floor, a nasty looking bump on the side of her head.

# CHAPTER 18

"Izzy?" I took a faltering step forward. The pressure in my head spiked. I scrambled to the entrance of the tunnel, my head swiveling from side to side.

Patricia stepped out from behind the curtains with a gun in her hand. She held it at her waist, pointing it straight at me.

"Hey, Patty." I held my hands out, palms facing her. "Let's just take a breath and think through things."

"Get back in the tunnel," Patricia said. Her voice was cold.

I swallowed. *If I go in, she's not going to let me back out.* I shook my head. "There are at least twenty people who know we came here."

"And if they ask, I'll testify that I saw you leave." Patricia took a step forward. "We're about the same height. I could drive your car out of here, so there would even be footage of you leaving to support my statement. Get in the tunnel. Now."

"No." I dropped my hands to my side.

Patricia whirled and pointed the gun at Izzy. "I said get in the tunnel."

"You don't look like Izzy. That blue hair is kind of distinctive," I said.

Patricia shook with rage. She stalked toward me and held the gun up, only a few inches from my face. "Get in the tunnel!"

A rock settled into my stomach. I forced myself to breathe normally. *I wish I hadn't dropped the pepper spray.* "We took separate cars. You would have to move both of them. How would you get back on the property without any of the cameras picking you up?"

Patricia inched forward. She was within arm's reach.

*Why didn't I stop to find it?* I ground my teeth and wobbled as the idea came to me. I had practiced the spell only a few times, but magic was mostly about need. And right then, I really needed that pepper spray.

I moved my hand behind my back and muttered the words to the summoning spell. *I need the pepper spray. Come to me.* I held the image of the canister in my head.

"What are you doing?" Patricia spluttered. "Praying won't help you."

I forced myself to concentrate on the spell. She would kill me the second I got in the tunnel, so the spell was my only hope. I continued to mutter the words under my breath. Motes of light flowed out of my mouth and disappeared behind me. *Please work. I need the pepper spray.*

"Stop it." Spittle formed at the edge of Patricia's mouth as she thrust the gun closer to my face. "Now."

My legs shook under me. I forced myself to breathe normally. The only way I had survived such situations in the past was to keep my wits about me. I couldn't run. Not yet. Izzy was, hopefully, just unconscious. I couldn't leave her there. I clenched my jaw and focused on the spell.

Patricia snarled and raised the gun over her head. I darted to the side and threw myself to the floor as her arm swung down. I scrambled behind the desk, desperately whispering the words to the spell. The motes of light continued to stream out of my mouth and into the tunnel. *Please.* Patricia stalked around the table toward me. I crawled backward on my hands and knees as the last words of the spell left my mouth.

"I could just say that I thought you were an intruder. You weren't supposed to be in here, after all." She grabbed me by my arm and yanked me to my feet. "If you get into the tunnel, I promise not to hurt your friend."

Patricia jerked me forward and pushed me toward the opening in the bookcases. I held my hands out to grab onto something, anything, to keep me in Edmund's office. A metallic object flew into my hand. I closed my fingers around it and flung myself away from her. She spun toward me, eyes wide with fury. I raised my hand and sprayed.

Patricia wailed and stumbled. She dropped the gun. A loud pop filled the air. Plaster on the far wall exploded outward, spraying the floor with white particles of dust. I kicked the gun away, and it skittered into the tunnel. I scrambled to Izzy and shook her.

Izzy groaned and opened one eye.

"We have to go." I wrapped my arm around her and hoisted her up from the ground.

Patricia clawed her face. "You're ruining everything."

I pulled Izzy to the door. She stumbled against me, half delirious.

"What's happening?" Izzy mumbled.

"We're running away." I yanked the door open and pushed Izzy out into the hall in front of me.

She shook her head and swayed in place.

I glanced over my shoulder. Patricia wiped her face, and her eyes were bloodshot. She glared at me and stepped toward the open tunnel entrance.

"Run!" I yelled and darted out the door before slamming it shut behind me.

I grabbed Izzy by the hand and sprinted down the hallway with her in tow. After she'd taken a few steps, her dizziness dissipated. She joined me stride for stride. We bolted down the hallway, through the sitting room, and into the foyer. Footsteps pounded behind us.

We burst out the front door and leaped down the porch steps. Izzy gasped for air as we ran toward my car. Another loud pop rang through the air. Chips of asphalt bounced up from the ground a foot to my left. I squealed and threw myself forward. I rolled behind my car and crouched behind the tires. Izzy scrambled around the car and slid to a stop next to me. She stared wide-eyed at me as I fumbled for my keys. Patricia reached the bottom of the steps, only a few feet from where we hid.

"Stop right where you are." Nelly rounded the corner of the house, holding a hunting rifle to her shoulder. She pointed the rifle at Patricia. "Drop the gun and put your hands up."

I pushed up to a crouching position and moved to the edge of the car. I peered over the hood.

Tony came to a stop next to Nelly. "Mom! What are you—"

Patricia turned toward Nelly, and she swung her gun arm up. I sprang to my feet and ran forward, barreling into her side and knocking her over. I pushed down on her with all my strength. My arms shook as she bucked against me and tried to twist the gun toward me.

Tony rushed forward and dropped to his knees next to me. He thrust his hands between us and grabbed the gun.

Patricia screeched and clung to the gun. My muscles screamed at me as I held her down. Tony twisted the gun and yanked it out of his mother's grasp. He tossed it away from him, into the grass. As it disappeared into the foliage, Patricia collapsed under me.

"What's wrong with you?" Tony stared at her in disbelief.

Patricia shook under me as she sobbed. "I was just trying to protect what's yours," she gasped.

Nelly inched forward, her rifle still pointed at Patricia. I backed away. Patricia wasn't going anywhere. She looked defeated.

Izzy stood from her hiding place next to my car, with her cellphone pressed to her ear. "Yes, at the Hastings estate. We got the gun away from her, but please send help."

"I did this for you," Patricia whispered as she reached for Tony.

He jerked his hand away and stood. He turned his back on her and wrapped his arms around himself. "I never asked you to."

Patricia sobbed as Nelly stood watch. I wrapped my arm around Izzy's shoulder, and we waited together until the sheriff's department arrived.

# CHAPTER 19

At the door, I stamped my boots to clear them of snow. A small flurry overnight had left a half-inch dusting of snow everywhere. The day was heating up, so it would be melted by noon. But I couldn't help feeling it was metaphorically wiping the slate clean. It had been only a day since my confrontation with Patricia, and it was already beginning to feel distant. Life had moved on. Insurance claims never stopped.

I glanced around the Slice of Life Diner as I shrugged out of my coat. Willow had spent the last few weeks changing the photos on the walls and regrouping them by area of town instead of by decade. I found Heather and Chris already waiting for me in the section dedicated to the pier. Photos ranging from the 1910s to the end of last year, when we had a Winter Intern Extravaganza, covered the wall above the booth.

I took a seat next to Chris. He bumped me with his leg under the table, and I wrapped my hand around his. My fingers tingled at the sudden temperature change. His hand was warm to the touch.

"Are you doing okay?" Heather asked, furrowing her brow.

I had texted her after the altercation with Patricia. She hadn't been pleased that another of my investigations had ended in a showdown. "I was shaken up yesterday, but today's been so normal that it almost feels like a dream, you know? I got home and then this morning went to work like any other day."

"I honestly don't know how you do that. If someone pointed a gun at me, I would be a basket case for at least a week." Heather lowered her voice. "What happened?"

Chris squeezed my hand under the table. A cool breeze swept through the room as the front door opened and closed behind me.

"I know it sounds morbid, but I wanted to get a photo of his office while—"

Izzy stepped up to the table next to me, clutching a newspaper. The right side of her face had a deep-bluish-purple bruise. Despite that, she wore a wide grin. She handed me the paper. "Sorry to interrupt. I saw you come in, and I just wanted to give you this."

I glanced at the paper. On the front page was a photo of the Hastings estate with a sheriff's car parked out front. The headline read, "Suspect Charged with the Murder of Edmund Hastings."

Izzy fidgeted with her hands and hovered awkwardly as I read and stared at the photo. It was one I had taken and texted her last night before bed. Her name was under the header, and mine, in small black text, was under the photo. It was surreal. Izzy cleared her throat and took a step back from the table. "Anyway, thanks again."

I glanced between her and the paper. She had been there almost every step of the way. "We were just talking about this. Would you like to join us?"

Izzy relaxed and slid into the booth across from me. "I would love to."

I handed the paper to Heather. "So while she"—I gestured to Izzy—"was finishing up her interview with Charlotte, I went into the office." I told them about discovering the secret door and our harrowing confrontation with a groundhog.

Willow stopped by the table to take our orders. Chris and I ordered slices of apple pie with vanilla ice cream and caramel sauce, while Heather got a brownie, and Izzy ordered fries with brown gravy. While the others ordered, Heather handed the newspaper to me, and I read the article. Izzy was a talented writer. The piece was somehow both professional and exciting. She captured the experience perfectly.

"How did you get Charlotte to approve this?" I asked after Willow had left.

Izzy preened. "I reminded my editor that Charlotte only had approval over the memorial piece. Not the murder investigation."

"So it's confirmed, then? Patricia killed Edmund?" I asked.

"She confessed this morning," Chris said. "After what she did to you guys, she couldn't hide anymore. Not really."

"How did she get out of the house? The tunnel was sealed," Izzy said.

"Unofficially?" Chris cocked an eyebrow.

Izzy threw up her hands. "Completely off the record. I'm just curious."

"She didn't." Chris relaxed into the bench. "She accessed the cameras from her phone and just waited until the coast was clear before coming out."

"Did she say why she did it?" Heather asked.

"Tony was Edmund's son," I said.

Chris nodded. "She got pregnant with his child while he was home for the holidays during college. His dad covered it up and made her keep it a secret, even from Edmund. When the will said an even split between Edmund's children, it meant that if he ever died, Anthony could still inherit something. She would just have to request a paternity test. But by giving each child something specific, she thought it would effectively cut him out."

"Did Anthony know?" Heather asked.

"Maybe. I think he suspected but didn't have it confirmed. Either way, he seems pretty shaken up by the whole thing," Chris said. "He's willing to testify about what he saw yesterday. But I can't help but feel for the guy."

"Me too. I can't imagine everyone finding out who your dad is that way." I sighed. "Or having to go through the awkwardness of the inheritance situation. I wonder if he's even going to assert his claim."

"If Lily has a say, I'm sure Edmund's family is going to fight him getting anything," Heather said as Willow stopped by the table to drop off our food.

"Maybe. It might be hard for them, though." Izzy dunked one of her fries into the gravy.

"Why's that?" I asked.

"I've heard from some reliable sources that Anthony was going to be included in the revised will," Izzy said.

I stared at her, wide-eyed. "So Patricia did it for nothing?"

"I wouldn't say for nothing," Izzy said. "He wasn't going to get part of the company, but he was going to get something. Enough that the average person would have financial security for life. I don't think Patricia knew about it, though. Charlotte sure didn't. From what I've heard, she's vacillating between livid and despondent. Edmund apparently found out he was Anthony's father a few months ago. Instead of telling her, he had a mini midlife crisis and decided to retire early and change his will. Reliable sources say it made him question his entire life. And he questioned it alone. Charlotte thought they were getting close but now sees that even in his final weeks, he was still keeping her at arm's length. She's currently going through the same crisis, except she gets to add being lied to for years by Patricia, someone she thought was her friend. She thinks her whole life has been a lie. A lie that is on public display."

"Wow." Heather slumped into her seat. "That's so sad."

We all nodded and ate our food in silence for a few minutes. I would do almost anything for my daughter, but I couldn't imagine killing anyone for her. She wouldn't want me to. Tony's life really had been turned upside down.

Izzy picked up her last french fry and swirled it around the gravy cup, scooping up the last vestiges of sauce. "Thanks again for working on this with me. I can understand why you like to get involved in these sorts of things."

I smiled. "It was nice working with you too."

"I worry about you when you get caught up in your investigations." Chris squeezed my hand. "Curiosity killed the cat, after all."

I squeezed his hand too. "And satisfaction brought it back."

We stood and paid at the counter. Izzy was the first one out the door. We followed her onto the sidewalk. The temperature was already rising, and the snow had become a thick sludge. Izzy bid us farewell and marched to her car. Heather followed suit, leaving Chris and me on the sidewalk alone.

I wrapped my arms around his waist and melted into his arms. I rested my head on his chest and breathed in his scent —cedar with a hint of vanilla underneath. I closed my eyes. "I've been meaning to thank you for your gift."

He nestled his chin against the top of my head and held me. "Oh?"

"The pepper spray helped me get away." I pulled back and stared up at him. His brown eyes crinkled at the corners. "I appreciate that you worry about me. I really do."

"I sense a *but* coming." He pushed a strand of my hair out of my face.

"No *but*. Just appreciation. You don't try to make me be something that I'm not." I stood on my tippy-toes and kissed him.

"You wouldn't be you if I made you change." He squeezed my hand and stepped back. "And you are pretty great."

"So are you." I giggled.

He lifted my hand to his lips and took another step back. "Alas. My lunch break is now over. Coffee tomorrow? I'll be on Millers Farm duty again."

"Sounds wonderful." I watched him as he strode to his car. He waved before driving away.

# CHAPTER 20

I spent the rest of the day completing damage reports and setting up inspections for the remainder of the week. Charlie sat at my desk while I typed, lounging behind my keyboard with a single paw sticking up in front of my monitor, blocking the clock. I periodically craned my neck over his foot to check the time. At five o'clock, I packed up and headed home for the night with Charlie in tow.

Grace's car was parked in the driveway when I got home. I idled next to it, staring at the house. We had barely spoken since our foray into Meredith's house. I chewed on my lip. Without a murder investigation to distract me, I didn't have an excuse not to research the curse anymore. I steeled myself, got out of the car, and strode toward the house with Charlie clutched to my chest for support. He nestled his head into my hair and purred into my ear.

I had taken the first step onto the porch stairs when the front door opened. Grace stood in the doorway, framed in the light from inside.

"I was beginning to think you weren't coming in," she said.

"Sorry." I shuffled past her, my mind whirling for an

excuse. "I got distracted. Izzy gave me a copy of the article she wrote."

"On the case?" Grace closed the door and flopped down onto the couch.

I nodded and fished the newspaper out of my bag. "According to Chris, Patricia gave a full confession."

"I'm glad things turned out okay." She took the paper from me and scanned the headline. "You know, I've always admired your desire to figure stuff out. I think I inherited the curiosity bug from you."

"Are you wanting to investigate murders now too?" I asked.

Charlie jumped from my arms to the couch and sat down next to Grace. He sat staring at me, his front paws placed perfectly in front of him.

"Maybe not murders. But all this witch stuff. The lessons I've been taking with Agnes have really been paying off. I could cast three spells today, which is more than I used to be able to manage."

I squeezed her shoulder and took a seat on the other end of the couch. "I'm proud of you."

"I really want to figure the curse out." She cleared her throat. "And that's why I need you to tell me about my grandmother."

I leaned forward and gripped the couch cushions. "There isn't anything to say—"

"If there was really nothing to say about her, you wouldn't be avoiding the question."

"I'm tired." I pushed myself up.

"If she knows something, it could help." Grace leaped to her feet. "She might have the answers to my nightmares. Or a clue we've missed. Why isn't it worth exploring?"

I peered at her out of the corner of my eye. She stood, her hands balled into fists. Her jaw was set. She wore the exact same expression she'd had when she fought to go back to track and field after she tore her ACL. I sighed and crumpled onto the couch. She had inherited her curiosity from me, but her stubbornness, she got from her father. Talking her out of anything was difficult.

"Lori… Lori wasn't a good mother," I began. "Growing up, she would take off periodically. Disappear for days, sometimes weeks at a time. It wasn't so bad when my dad was around. But after they split, I had to learn how to take the train up here whenever she was gone too long."

"Mom…" Grace sank to the couch, her hand half covering her mouth.

Charlie head-butted my arm and wormed his way onto my lap.

"When I graduated from high school and went off to college, she became stable finally. She showed up to the parents' weekend. When I got pregnant with you my senior year, she moved closer, and we saw each other every weekend. She came to every doctor's appointment. Every parenting class. She helped with the baby shower. She built your crib. For the first time, my mother was part of my life."

I stared up at the photo over the mantel. Me, my gran, and my mom smiled down at us. I was bloated from the pregnancy, but there was joy on all our faces. I blinked back a tear and hugged Charlie to my chest.

"What happened?" Grace whispered.

"When I graduated, I got a job working in insurance. I didn't have a lot of time saved up, so I had to go back to work. Ed took as much time off as he could. But there was a single day, one single day, where we needed a babysitter before you could start at day care, and we were both out of time off from work. Lori volunteered. She had been so good for so long, I almost forgot how unreliable she was growing up, so I said yes."

Grace sat there quietly, waiting for me to finish.

"I got home first. When I got there, I could hear you

screaming from the street. And I just knew something was wrong." I buried my face into Charlie's fur. "I ran inside and sprinted to your room. You were in your crib. It was clear you had been alone for hours. You hadn't been fed or changed. And Lori was nowhere to be found."

Grace squeezed my shoulders. "Did she ever say why?"

"I called her. I texted her. She didn't respond, and after twenty-four hours, I called the cops. I thought something had happened. They found her and confirmed that she was okay." I choked. "And that was it. She never reached out to me again. And eighteen years of no contact is a long time."

Grace swiveled and crouched in front of me. "I can't imagine how that must have felt."

"I thought I would have gotten used to it by then. You know?" I cried. "She left so often. I can't figure out why it surprised me when she did it again."

"It's okay." She pulled me into a hug, with Charlie between us. "I'm with you for the long haul. And so is Charlie. We're not going to leave you like she did."

"I know." I pulled back, wiping my eyes.

"Do you?" She picked up Charlie and lifted him until he was staring into my eyes. "Then why haven't you tried to cast the Familiar spell yet?"

"What if it isn't him?" I spoke my fear out loud.

"Then he will still love you." She pushed him into my arms. "And have a friend."

I held Charlie to my chest. He wiggled until his paws were over my shoulder and made biscuits on my jacket.

"All right." I scratched him behind the ears. "I'll do it."

Grace stood and retrieved the spell book. She flipped it open to the last page and held it up for me to read. It amazed me how many spells used household items. I stood, and Grace followed me into the kitchen. She placed the book on the counter, and I set Charlie next to it. He watched as we gathered the items.

We still had mugwort and wild bergamot from when Agnes was there. The cinnamon, bay leaves, and dandelion petals were already in our kitchen cupboards. I ground the herbs together while Grace fetched coals from our camping gear and started the grill. The spell called for burning the herbs and inhaling the smoke while the witch meditated. The grill was the best way to make sure it burned slowly enough, at least with what we had available in the house.

I ground the last of the ingredients together and carried them down to the daylight basement. We huddled on the back porch and waited for the grill to heat up. I gripped the herb-filled mortar, my hands shaking as I stepped up to the grill.

"Could you hold the book so I can see it?" I asked.

Grace stepped up to the grill. She took a position on the opposite side and held the book there. I read the words of the spell as I sprinkled the mixture over the grill. The tiny pieces of petals singed, and a woody scent filled the air. I continued to murmur the words as I sprinkled more and more of the mixture onto the grill. Motes of white light floated out of my mouth and swirled around the coals. The lights danced between me and the smoke. I relaxed my eyes as the words continued to pour out of my mouth. *Please be Charlie. Let me find my Familiar, but please be Charlie.* The lights spiraled faster and faster until all I could see was the light and the grill. It surrounded me, infusing the air, filling my lungs.

The lights froze then surged through my chest. I spun in place, following the light. The lights flew into the house, streaking between my chest and Charlie.

I gasped.

Though I had always felt a connection to him, this was like nothing I had ever experienced before. I was keenly aware of where he was. It was almost as if I could feel the concrete beneath his paws and see myself staring down at him. I drifted toward him. He stood and jumped into my arms. The second we touched, the lights flashed then went out, leaving us in darkness. But somehow, I could still see.

Laughing, I clutched him to my chest. It wasn't that he could suddenly talk. But I could understand him somehow. I could sense him. And he could sense me. He was so happy to be in my arms, and I knew it. I knew it like I knew my own mind. My heart swelled with love. I was never going to feel alone again.

---

Can't wait for the next book? Book 5, 'Spells and the Suspiciously Silent,' will be coming out October 15, 2024. You can pre-order it by scanning the QR code below, and be the first to uncover the next magical mystery in the 'A Williams Witch Mystery' series.

In book 5, Dani Williams is shocked when a break-in at Abby's Bistro leads to the discovery of a body amidst the wreckage. The police quickly zero in on Abby as a person of interest after she's seen fleeing the scene. Determined to clear Abby's name, Dani dives headfirst into an investigation.

But this case is unlike any Dani has faced before. When using her abilities, she usually uncovers emotional imprints left behind by the perpetrator. This time, she finds nothing. It's as if the killer is a ghost. Finding herself in uncharted territory, she has to navigate a web of secrets and deception blind. Every clue leads to a dead end, and every lead seems to vanish into thin air.

With Abby's freedom hanging in the balance, Dani must rely on her wit, determination, and the support of her friends to piece together the puzzle. Can she unravel the mystery in time to save Abby, or will the elusive killer slip through her fingers?

Join her in this spellbinding journey of magic, mystery, and the strength of true friendship in the latest installment of this captivating paranormal cozy mystery series.

## JOIN MY NEWSLETTER

Interested in receiving bonus content like inspiration character art or a free short story? If so, scan the QR code below to become a member of my mailing list and receive access to fun things like 'Foresight and the Fateful Ferry,' a free short story. Go on an adventure with Dani and Chris as they journey to Seattle for a fun day out, and things take a dramatic turn when they stumble upon a dead body on the ferry.

# ABOUT THE AUTHOR

Eloise Everhart lives in the Pacific Northwest. Her childhood was marked by voracious reading and tabletop roleplaying games, fueling her lifelong passion for storytelling.

By day, she's a dedicated insurance adjuster. It's a career that has honed her sharp eye for detail and developed her inquisitive mind—a skillset she now seamlessly integrates into her cozy mystery writing.

Beyond her storytelling ardor, Eloise is a devoted wife, sharing her home with a menagerie of rescued cats and dogs who have found their furever home in the Everhart household.

[f]

# ACKNOWLEDGMENTS

I would like to extend my heartfelt thanks to my editors, Rashida Breen and Angela McRae, for their invaluable assistance in helping me weave the threads of this story together. Your insights and dedication have been instrumental in bringing this book to life.

To my husband, Nate, your unwavering support and encouragement have been my anchor. Thank you for always standing by my side through every step of this journey.

My deepest gratitude goes to my sister, Andrea, and my parents, Chas and Tammy. Your love and encouragement in my formative years inspired me to embrace my creativity, and I am forever thankful for that foundation.

And as always, I would like to honor my best friend, Andrew, who is no longer with us. You were my guiding light through tough times, and your memory continues to inspire and motivate me.

"Come on a journey with me."

www.ingramcontent.com/pod-product-compliance
Lightning Source LLC
Chambersburg PA
CBHW021959190626
46808CB00017B/2576